CASEBOOK
OF A
PRIVATE
(Cat's)
EYE

CASEBOOK
OF A
PRIVATE
(Cat's)
EYE

Mary Stolz

illustrated by Pamela R. Levy

Front Street/Cricket Books
Chicago

A previous version of this story appeared in *Cricket* magazine.

———————————

Text copyright © 1999 by Mary Stolz
Illustrations copyright © 1999 by Pamela R. Levy
All rights reserved
Library of Congress Catalog Card Number: 98-88521
Printed in the United States of America
Designed by Ron McCutchan
Second printing, 2000

For Margie and Bob Sokol,
our dear, our very dear friends
—M. S.

For Eloise
—P. R. L.

Eileen O'Kelly, Private Investigator

My office, which I opened early in this year of 1912, is in an old West End brownstone, a block from the boardinghouse where I room. On the office door, in gold-colored lettering, is a sign that reads:

EILEEN O'KELLY
PRIVATE INVESTIGATOR

DISCREET INQUIRIES CONDUCTED

So far as I know, I am the only female, feline private detective in Boston—possibly in the United States— maybe (who knows?) in the world. With but a few months at my calling, business is not brisk and my days offer too much spare time.

So—I read a lot.

I have been following the exploits of Sherlock Holmes, the famous British sleuth. His successes in the world of crime are described and presented to the public by his associate, Dr. John Watson. I understand these volumes are lucrative. That is to say, they make money. Until my career gets on a sounder footing, I am a cat in need of money.

Therefore I have decided to offer for publication a selection of my cases, serving as my own Dr. Watson. As getting enough pages to fill a book is important, I shall include all manner of investigations, large and small, short and lengthy. So far, all I have is a title:

CASEBOOK OF A PRIVATE (CAT'S) EYE

Cat-chy, I think. My hope is that it will engage the public fancy and so provide an improvement on my still rather paw-to-mouth existence.

While waiting for clients, I occupy my time with reading, yawning, polishing my claws, and general grooming. I also flip a feather duster about, then pass, alas, too much time at the window, watching activities in a field across the way.

My small office is attractive. In season, my window boxes are filled with flowers. I have a bright rug, a few choice pictures, and a wicker tea wagon upon which is a really nice porcelain tea set. I got all of this at a pawn-shop a few blocks off the Boston Common.

My neighbor across the hall makes hats. Her name is Bertha Forbes, but the sign on her door (done by the same fancy letterer who did mine) reads:

MADAME ZORINA, Milliner

This morning, tired of my own company, I went across to see if she was free to talk, or take tea, or go for a walk.

Madame Zorina's large room is entirely filled with hats finished, hats in preparation, and sketches on a drawing board of hats to come. On a wide shelf stand wooden heads, some bald, some wearing fanciful creations in the chapeau line. Tables and shelves are piled and crowded with a dazzling collection of ribbons—waxed and unwaxed—voiles, rosettes, plumes, sequins, veilings, yards of straw batting, rolls of buckram, boxes of silk and cotton and paper flowers.

The place is so crowded with trade necessities that Bertha has but one chair, and that for herself. Customers sit on a high stool in front of a full-length mirror.

"Madame Zorina," said I from the doorway, "will you step across the hall and take a dish of tea?"

We laughed. "Taking a dish of tea" is an English expression that has made its way into Boston society, which likes to consider itself more British than American.

"With pleasure, deary," she said. "Be with you as soon as I stick a finishing feather on this chapeau for Mrs. Avery Johnstone III."

"Oh my," said I. "You do attract a glossy clientele."

"Can you wonder? Regard!"

She held up for my inspection a simply enormous hat of complicated elegance. A bronzy shade of velvet, very broad-brimmed, high-crowned, piles of veiling, oodles of waxed ribbon, and a perfect fountain of scarlet and green feathers from what unfortunate bird I could not tell.

"It is splendid. Sumptuous," I said, then added, "I cannot imagine actually *wearing* it."

Bertha laughed. "The ladies who come to me have nothing to do but swan about Boston in drawing rooms

and ballrooms, opera and concert houses, each of them trying to outdo all the others in the matter of dress."

"I do not think you will remain much longer in this old building," I said with regret. Word of her artistry having reached as far as Mrs. Avery Johnstone III, Bertha will surely move to quarters more commodious and chic.

She made no answer, merely twirled the hat on one paw with an expression of perfect satisfaction. It seemed to confirm my speculation that a move was not far off.

I shall miss her.

After tea, Bertha proposed a walk. We are both great walkers, in meadows, along woodland trails, sometimes strolling the interesting, historic streets of Boston and Cambridge.

Today, as Mrs. Avery Johnstone III was due for a fitting later that afternoon, we elected to go no farther than the neighboring field I mentioned earlier.

It provides a pleasing saunter at any time of year, with a vast expanse of grass and wildflowers in summer, large shade trees to shelter one from the heat, and a pond where in spring, summer, and early autumn, cat families row in small boats, and kittens and young cats cavort near the shore. Come winter, the pond freezes over and turns into a great ice rink where cats of all ages and breeds skate, singly, in groups, or—I eye these wistfully—in couples. There are even fancy sleighs drawn by high-stepping horses, bells a-jingle. As darkness draws in, strings of colored lanterns illuminate the scene. A merry, fairyland sight it is then.

Today I counted three softball games going on, no girls allowed. I watched a group of boys batting, running the bases, tumbling, sliding, shouting, tearing their clothes, getting *dirty*.

"Did you ever wish, when you were a girl, that you could join the boys in their games?" I asked.

"Mercy, no! I simply could not abide boys, *or* their games. Still cannot."

"You were content just to play with dolls?"

"Play with them, dress them, give them tea parties, put them to bed in their lacy little nightgowns. I made all their clothes myself. Oh, I simply loved my dollies. Did not you, Eileen?"

"No! I wanted to play ball in summer and have snowball fights in winter."

"You were a tomboy!" she exclaimed.

"I guess so. I know I envied boys. I hated the way my brothers were so free and wild. Just look at those fellows over there in their knickers and sweaters. They don't have to worry about keeping their clothes nice and neat."

"Frightful," Bertha murmured, shaking her head in disapproval.

Ignoring that, I pointed toward a group of girls sitting in a circle on the grass. They were playing school, teaching their dolls to behave nicely. To stay nice and neat.

"You call that *playing?*" I asked.

"They seem happy. Don't you think girls like to be tidy and pretty? I did, when I was their age." Bertha glanced again at the ball game. "Eileen, surely you didn't want to be such a *rowdy.* So messy. So noisy."

Still looking at the girls and their dolls, I said, "It's all the fault of our clothes."

"What fault?"

"Bertha! Watch how those boys can play! They can run and tumble and have *fun!* Now look at the girls. Look at their *garments,* will you? Swathed and smothered and layered in petticoats and flouncy skirts and thick cotton stockings. They're even wearing *bonnets!* On a day like this!"

Bertha, turning her head slightly, studied the group. "Not one of them really pretty. I do not mean the girls themselves. They're pretty enough. But such dreary outfits! As for those bonnets . . . my dear, the only word is *indescribable!*"

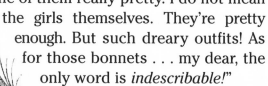

"That's what I've been trying to say! Oh, I wish Amelia Bloomer's trouser outfits for ladies had become the fashion!"

"If I had been devising her atrocity," Bertha mused, "I should not have made the pants so balloonlike. I'd have cut them like men's trousers, trim and narrow. But, of course, I deplore the whole notion of 'bloomers,' as people call them."

"I don't. What heaven—to be free of all these tiers of fabrics, all the laws about seemly appearance and behavior."

"Ah, Eileen," said Bertha with a laugh. "I recall the adorable skating costume you wore last winter. Then you didn't mind tiers of clothing, not at all! All you minded was the gentleman in the checkered suit who failed to notice you."

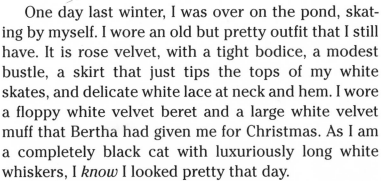

One day last winter, I was over on the pond, skating by myself. I wore an old but pretty outfit that I still have. It is rose velvet, with a tight bodice, a modest bustle, a skirt that just tips the tops of my white skates, and delicate white lace at neck and hem. I wore a floppy white velvet beret and a large white velvet muff that Bertha had given me for Christmas. As I am a completely black cat with luxuriously long white whiskers, I *know* I looked pretty that day.

There I was, perfectly happy with my own company, happy, too, with my costume—Bertha was right about that—when a gentleman wearing a checkered suit, a black bowler hat, and a scarlet scarf appeared on the ice. I watched, entranced, as he flew across the frozen pond, bent over a little, head down, hands behind him, swooping, bounding, soaring in arcs, sending off sparks of such joy that it was joyous to see him.

He sailed past several times without seeing me.

Well! Enough of the past.

   *   *   *

Bertha and I returned to the brownstone, she to keep her appointment with Mrs. Avery Johnstone III, I to await the arrival of a client.

Any client.

2

The Lox Caper

At two o'clock I heard Mrs. Avery Johnstone III climb the stairs and knock genteelly at Bertha's door. Shortly afterward, someone else mounted the stairs and pounded, in no way genteelly, at my door. It was the owner of Herbie's General Dry Goods and Grocery Store. He sat in one of my two visitors' chairs, put his hat on his lap, and snapped, "My stock of lox is constantly diminishing."

Lox, as I knew, was a salty salmon, frequently served with capers, a tasty species of pickled flower buds.

"Something must be done!" Mr. Herbie growled. "Are you free to start work immediately?"

I opened a ledger I keep on the desk, saying, "I shall have to consult my book."

"See here, Miss O'Kelly, I came to you because I thought, being a woman, you'd not be very busy."

Alas, I am too much in need of work to have risked the proper retort.

Besides, from my brief—so far—professional experience, I know that every person thinks his, or her, problem matters more than anything else going on in Boston. Or outside of it, for the matter of that. "Me, me, me! Put me first!" they all but say, and some of them do say. Still, it is natural that they should feel so. After all, what is more vital to any of us than "Me, me, me"?

"As it happens," I said, closing the ledger, "I am free now. If you'll explain a bit further?"

"Explain? I just told you—my lox stock is going down markedly, in a way I cannot account for. Not through *sales,* look you," he added vexedly.

"How, then?"

"That's what I am asking you to find out! That's why I am here!"

"Mice?" I suggested.

"We do not have mice!" he declared. "Not in *my* establishment."

I could have told him that everybody has mice, and especially do dry goods and grocery stores have mice. But the little imps are so canny that scarcely anyone sees them. Certainly I wouldn't rat on them. I like mice. That may seem an ambiguous statement, but I shall not elaborate.

I reported to Mr. Herbie's establishment early the next morning as promised and spent the next few days crouching at the many mouseholes he was unaware of. They were mostly in the back storeroom, behind bales of dry goods, barrels of pickles, boxes and crates of whatever he kept there. I didn't pay much attention, except to the mouseholes.

The relationship between cat and mouse is a waiting game, and mousehole watching requires skill. It is something a detective either has or she quickly goes broke. I have it. Patience, endless patience is required, and an ability to maintain hours of immobility. I moved quietly from hole to hole, maintaining an almost cataleptic watch for hours at a time.

Mr. Herbie began to get restless.

"What are you doing in my storeroom all the time?" he demanded after nearly a week had passed. "Why do you just sit in there behind barrels and boxes, doing nothing, wasting my time? I'm not paying you to do nothing, look you."

He hadn't, in fact, paid me anything, having firmly refused to give an advance. There'll come a day when I won't have to take this high-handed attitude from anyone. But that day is not in sight yet, so I'd agreed to take payment on condition of success. Mr. Herbie had *not* endeared himself to me.

On the occasion when he reproached me for wasting time, I fixed him with a severe eye and said, "Mr. Herbie, I go about my business in the way I think best. I am, after all, a professional. If you feel another detective would fare better, do please say so. And pay me for the days I have put in so far."

"Pay you for—," he sputtered. "I said I'd pay when you find the thief!" He threw up his paws. "I *suppose* you know what you're doing. Despite appearances. It's just that the lox supply is still diminishing, and you—"

"Give me another day. Then, if my hunch is wrong, we'll settle the matter of payment."

He began to protest, frowned, turned, and walked away.

After he left, a little mouse appeared at a hole directly behind a pile of shoeboxes, and a little mouse voice squeaked at me. "Listen, Cat—we want to know something."

"Who is we?"

"Me and my family and friends back here. We want to know are you taking up residence in this place? Has he gone and got himself a cat to hound us mice?"

I leaned nearer the hole, and the nose disappeared.

Backing away a bit, I said gently, "No, no, no. That's not the case. I mean, it's not *my* case. That is—you see, I am a detective. The only female feline private eye in Boston."

"Never heard of such a thing," said the tiny voice from a distance.

"Do please come closer," I said. "I've no wish in the world to harm you and your family and friends. I *like* mice."

"Do you, now?" he said in a skeptical squeak.

"Well, let's not argue. I was hired to find out why Mr. Herbie keeps losing his lox."

"Oh, that." The little fellow had his whole head out of the hole by now. "I can tell you that."

"You can!" I sputtered. "That is, *will* you? I'd be ever so grateful."

"H'm. Grateful enough to warn those cats who prowl around the backyard to leave us mice alone?"

"Well, of *course* I'll do that. Whether they'll pay attention to me—"

"Do your best." The mouse's nose suddenly twitched. "Now you just keep your eyes open, and you will see what you will see."

Just then the door to the storeroom opened, and the delivery boy, a skinny tabby, came in with a wooden box on his shoulder. He lowered it carefully to the floor, and I saw the stencil on the side, plain as plain.

Finest Oregon Lox!!!

The tabby peeked into the outer room to be sure Mr. Herbie was occupied. Then, taking a screwdriver from his apron pocket, he quietly went to work and got the lid off the box, laid it gently aside, and extracted a thick shining slice of lox. The aroma almost put me in a swoon.

He put his prize in a bag, clearly brought for the purpose—a foresighted thief—stowed it in his apron pocket, deftly rearranged the wrapping in the box so that it appeared undisturbed, screwed the lid back on, and put the screwdriver in his pocket. Then, suave as you please, whistling a little, he strode toward the front of the store, calling out, "Here's the week's delivery of lox, Uncle! Right on time!"

"Well!" said I aloud. "What do you know!"

"Told you," came a squeak from the hole behind the shoeboxes. "You should've asked the first day."

"But I didn't know you were there. Besides, if a case gets solved too fast, the client thinks it was so easy he could've done it himself. I can't have that, can I?"

"Just remember your promise," he said and retreated down his tunnel on little skittering claws.

"I shall," I promised, though by then he was probably out of earshot.

It developed that Mr. Herbie's nephew had become sadly dependent upon lox. He had turned to crime to satisfy his craving. I was sorry for him, but after all I had—so to speak—discovered the culprit and was therefore due my fee. Would you believe it, Mr. Herbie

tried to question my demand! He said I was asking too much for what I'd done, and that by exposing his nephew in this fashion, I'd disgraced his family and really shouldn't get a penny.

Ha!

I may look like a dainty black feline with extraordinarily long white whiskers. But I am tough in tooth and claw. If not, I'd be in some other line of work. Mr. Herbie paid the full amount I asked. Spot cash. On the spot. I won't put up with welshers.

I left him to deal with his nephew, went to the backyard, and asked a big gray cat who was sunning on the bricks if he and the other cats would leave the mice in the dry goods and grocery store alone, as they were friends of mine.

He opened his amber eyes, fixed them on my green ones, yawned, and said, "Oh, *sure.* Anything you say, lady."

He was asleep in a wink.

I had kept my promise and could not do more.

Case concluded

3

Lost!
A Grand Slam Baseball

On a sultry day in July, I was alone in the office, combing my tail, when a brawny, brawly-looking brown tiger cat, who must've weighed twenty pounds, came hurtling into the office like a runner sliding into second under the tag. He sat across from my desk, lit a cigar without asking permission, and roared at me, "I'm Smokey Jack Slattery."

"How may I help you, Mr. Slattery?" I asked, waving a paw at the fumes, thinking chances were slim that he and I would get together on anything.

His ears flattened. A bad sign in any cat. "Sister, are you kiddin'? Ya claim ya never *heard* a' me?"

"Well, perhaps—," I murmured.

I did know who he was, had even seen him pitch a no-hitter, but thought a bit of comeuppance would do him good. I shrugged, as if giving up on his identity.

"Ha! Calls herself a private eye! Lives in Boston!

And don't know who Smokey Jack Slattery is?" He shook his big head and started from the chair. "I guess I better scare up a gumshoe knows what's goin' on in this here world."

"As you wish," I said, wondering why a roughneck like this would come to me in the first place.

He sat back, scowling, ears flattening.

"I twirl for the Furway Bobcats. Not to make a song and dance of it, but I'm their ace lefty. We don't have an ace right-hander. Couple a' fireballers that're pretty good, and a couple a' finesse pitchers—"

"I gather you are a baseball player?"

He jumped to his feet.

"Sister, you oughta go into some other line a' work. Alla Boston loves the Bobcats, who are one day gonna win the World Series, for cat almighty's sake, if we ever get a right-hander can find the plate without the catcher carries it halfway to the mound and an outfield that stops runnin' in place! Alla Boston knows we can do it!"

"It seems you have a way to go," I said, and added, "No, no, Mr. Slattery. Don't take offense. Sit down. There, that's better. Now then—why did you come to me? There are tomcat private eyes available. You look like a man who'd prefer to deal with men. That is," I added, "in matters of business."

"I sure would." He looked around my office, curling his lip, showing strong white teeth. "Fancy-dancey, ain't we?"

"I try to stay a step above slovenly."

"How the—how d'ya stay in business, is what I wanna know, talkin' like that to customers? *If* I was a customer. Which I ain't."

"I prefer the word 'client,'" I told him. "My *clients*

must take me as they find me. Otherwise—" I looked at the door. "They are free to go elsewhere."

"Like I say, how the—heck—do you stay in business with a tongue like yours?"

I regarded him in silence.

After a moment, he sighed and said, "You know anythin' at all about baseball?"

"I can tell a bat from a backstop."

Actually, I had had a beau a few months back, Shane Finley, a patrolman in the Boston City Police Department, who was crazy about the game. He had two topics of conversation. Would he ever make sergeant . . . and baseball. It was interesting to me, during the time I was walking out with him, to hear about police procedure, giving me an opportunity to pick up some professional tips.

Box scores, batting averages, and slugging percentages could be tiresome, but I found that I enjoyed watching the game itself on the several occasions when

I went with Shane to Furway Park. Baseball is a beautiful sport. Graceful, spacious, rich in tradition.

However, Shane Finley's two topics got on my nerves. Now and then, I would have liked to speak of clouds, or cabbages, or poetry. Or even—for goodness sakes—something of my own work. My career. But that was something Shane disapproved of. Once he referred to me, with a snicker, in front of others, as "me friend, the lady gumshoe." I told him not to call me that again. He called me that again. I don't walk out with Shane Finley anymore. And I'll be surprised if he ever makes sergeant.

But I hear things, even when I'm not listening. It's one reason why I am a good sleuth. I learned something of baseball from the baseball-mad patrolman. I knew that Smokey Jack was a southpaw with a blazing fastball, a good move to first, and a fadeaway pitch that left batters spinning at the plate like tops.

"Look, sister," he was saying now. "You gotta find me lucky baseball, you get that?"

"Don't call me sister, you get that? To you, to my clients, *if* you become one, I am Miss O'Kelly."

We stared at each other for a long minute, and then I said, "Why do we not try to understand the situation? You said something about a lucky baseball?"

He leaned forward and began to speak in a hoarse and urgent tone. "It's like this, see. Last month, first time in me whole entire life and it's never gonna happen again—you could bet your last bag a' catnip on that—I connected!"

"With what?"

He grabbed his head with both paws and shook it, glaring as if driven to distraction.

"I hit it! Clear outta Furway! With the sacks full!"

"Hit what? Sacks of what?" Foolish to bait a potential client. But he was so excitable. He was so LOUD.

He scowled, growled, made a move to rise, sat back, and studied my face. "I think you know darn well what I hit outta the park, sist—Miss O'Kelly. I think you know it wasn't no pot cozy." He glanced at my tea wagon.

"Very well." Any more teasing, I'd lose him for sure. "You hit it out of the park, with the bases loaded. It does happen. Not often, I grant."

"Are you nuts! I tole you! I'm a *pitcher,* for cat's

sake! How many times is a pitcher gonna hit a grand slam? Never! That's how many times!"

"You just said you did."

He slumped, as if suddenly tired. "Yeah. Well, anyways. So I hit it outta Furway, which not even sluggers do as an everyday thing. And it lands in the street. Only where? Everybody in the whole a' Boston knows what I did." He looked at me morosely. "I bet even you knew—"

"I might've heard."

"And so everybody—*everybody*—in Bean Town knows how I want that ball back. How I just gotta get it back! I need it. I need it in the worst way. I wanna see it perched on me mantelpiece, maybe gold-plated. You see what I'm sayin'? It's me good-luck piece, and without it, I'm outta luck—outta *luck*—you get that? I get that ball back, me fastball'll come back." Again he leaned forward. "Between just the two of us, and I *mean* that—I'm beginnin' to lose me stuff."

"Don't your teammates suspect? Your manager? Even—the fans?"

He showed those teeth, and back went the ears. "I din't say it *shows.* It's a thing I just feel. In here." He thumped his great chest. "Keep it in mind, you're the only one knows. I don't want you to forget that, not for one minute."

"What have you done so far to try to find it? The ball, I mean." I certainly didn't mean his "stuff." With a couple of miracle exceptions, once a pitcher begins to lose his stuff, he keeps on losing till it's gone. And then he's gone. That's how the game goes.

"Well, see—I advertised in the papers. Put fliers on lampposts. Tole everybody and his brother to keep their eyes peeled. I done everythin' I could think of to get that ball back, because somebody somewheres has *got* it. That ball din't melt like a ice-cream cone. It's gotta be *somewheres,* and I *gotta get it back.*"

This "get it back" litany was beginning to be tiresome, but I had decided I wanted his case. It would be a challenge. "You searched the area just outside the park? Where it would have fallen?"

"Ah—a' course we done that. Me and some of the guys scoured every inch, and it wasn't to be found. Well, what d'ya expect? A ball comes flyin' outta the park, a horde a' kids is on it pronto."

"So?"

"So somebody *took* it. And ain't gonna give it back without a fight. Or cash. I'm ready to pay any amount. Practically. I don't have what you'd call a treasure trove."

"I still wonder—why did you come to me, instead of to—well, someone else?"

He scratched his ear, appeared to consider, then said quickly, as if to get it over with, "Me mum, God rest her, always found stuff when I lost it. I was forever losin' stuff. I don't mean—I mean, stuff like *things,* see. Not the sort a'—"

He broke off, muddled between stuff like *things* and the stuff he displayed on the mound. Sighing hugely, he pressed on. "So whatever I lost, me mum would go look in a certain spot, and there it would be!"

"The things you'd misplaced."

"I din't misplace things. I plain lost them. And every time, whatever it was, me mum could find it. 'Struth, so help me."

I was looking at him in disbelief. Was I supposed to replace Mum, God rest her, in the lost-and-found department?

"So," he was going on, "I was walkin' past this here buildin' and seen your sign, and I says to meself, *That's a sign!* This lady's got the same name, Eileen, as me sainted mother, and so maybe she can find things for me, too. Like Mum did," he explained anxiously, as if I had not understood.

He sat back, having made a sensible explanation of a straightforward situation. His mother, Eileen, had found lost toys when he was a boy, and doubtless misplaced keys and collar buttons and currency and the dear knows what else when he was a young man. Only now Mum was gone, and here was I, with her same—hardly uncommon—name, about to be her replacement in the matter of his missing baseball and his failing fastball.

Goodness! thought I. *What* a challenge!

"Mr. Slattery," I said, "I shall do all in my power to solve your problem."

"I knew it!" he said, tears gathering in his very blue eyes. "I knew it was a sign that I could count on you, Eileen."

Clearly I was not going to be Miss O'Kelly to this client, but I didn't insist, merely saying that I'd be in touch when there was anything to report.

"You won't be mindin', now, if I stop around from time to time, just to see how you're comin' along?"

Having people "stop around" is inconvenient, and I'd be minding a good deal. But I know an immovable object when I meet it.

"I shall have to ask for an advance," I said.

"Oh, sure. Sure thing—" He poked a fistful of bills at me without counting. I had difficulty making him wait until I'd taken what I wanted and given him a receipt.

What an assignment! Find the needle in the

haystack. Find a baseball in Boston. Neither offered a promising prospect, but I was surely willing to try.

Case pending

4

Murder
Most Unsavory

Maybe Smokey Jack Slattery was *my* good-luck charm, because after he paid his visit, business began to pick up. A week later, on a morning in early August, a beautiful calico cat came to see me. She was dressed in mourning, even to a fringed ebony silk parasol. A faint minty scent hovered about her, and she kept touching her eyes with a sheer linen handkerchief, bordered with black lace.

She sat across the desk from me and sobbed, "I am here about my sister, my darling sister, Jewel. She was *murdered.* That was over three months ago, and the police are getting nowhere. Her killer must be found! I come to you as a last resort."

I scarcely fancied that remark, but overlooked it as she was clearly desperate. Of course I knew who she was. Miss Clara Ramsey, who kept the famous Inn on Nashua Street, noted for its comfortable atmosphere, fine antique furnishings, and superb cuisine. Before the murder, she and her sister had operated the establishment together.

Miss Jewel's murder had been in all the papers. A front-page sensation at first, it was gradually moved to the back of the second section. When no progress was made toward finding the felon, the public lost interest and, therefore, so did the newspapers.

Naturally, fresh leads would always revive public and publishing appetites, and apparently Clara Ramsey hoped that I could unearth these fresh leads. In spite of her distress, I found the prospect of working on a murder case thrilling.

How sad it is that unless it strikes very close to home, we cannot truly share another's grief or terror.

I waited until Miss Clara had sobbed herself into silence, then inquired what she hoped I could do that the police had not.

She blinked at fresh tears. "They say they never forget a murder and still have men on it, but nothing *happens*. And I cannot see that they're doing a single thing anymore. It is all so terribly hard on me. I keep seeing her . . . *lying* there!" Her sobs increased.

"Would you like a cup of tea?" I suggested, hoping to divert her, for a moment, from the memory of a scene so dreadful. I'd have to bring her back to it, but thought a respite might be useful.

As if she'd not heard, she continued, "They aren't looking for clues, or at least not at the Inn anymore. I just don't know what they *are* doing, except keeping that copper out front at night. Conrad's a better watchdog."

"Conrad?"

"Our goose. For goodness sakes, don't you know anything? *Everybody's* heard of our guard goose, Conrad."

"Oh yes, of course."

I recalled talk of a ferocious goose who patrolled the grounds of the Inn on Nashua Street at night. Apparently he was able to distinguish guests from interlopers and behave accordingly.

"I wonder," said I, "how a—how such a fiend could have gotten into the Inn that night with Conrad on duty. It was at night that your—that the crime took place?"

"Oh yes, yes," she moaned. "Somebody knocked Conrad out, I can't think how. He is always the attacker, not the attacked. Except that night . . . except that night . . . Oh, dear! Perhaps I shall accept your offer of tea."

I busied myself at the cart, deciding how to proceed. This was, or could be, my most important case by far. I put my best efforts into all my cases, of course. Still, to a detective, homicide is the supreme challenge.

Over our teacups and shortbread biscuits, I questioned her, as gently as possible.

"It was you, was it not, who found your . . . ah . . . who found the . . ."

"The body," she said harshly. "Yes, I found my dear Jewel, in the parlor, in the morning, lying on the floor." She closed her eyes. "I cannot get it out of my mind. I never shall."

"How was Conrad knocked unconscious?"

"The police say with a rock, expertly thrown. It would have to be, because that goose has been ducking, as it were—" she gave the faintest of smiles "—missiles of one kind or another for years. He must, for the first and only time, have failed to remain alert."

"But he has recovered?"

"Oh yes. He's well again, back on the job. I don't think he fully realizes what a dreadful cost his inattention

brought upon us. He's such a loyal bird. Irreplaceable."
After this generous tribute, she thought further and
added, "Maybe he's getting past the job, stupid creature."

She was certainly a capricious cat.

"Now then," I said briskly. "To business! According
to the papers, a valuable cookery book is missing. As
the food at the Inn on Nashua Street is famous
throughout New England and beyond, I must conclude
that the loss of these recipes has a bearing on the
case. Who is your chef?"

"Why," she exclaimed in astonishment, "*Jewel* was!
I thought everybody knew that. I do begin to wonder,
Miss O'Kelly, if you are right for this job . . ."

"Of course," I said stiffly, "you must be the one to
decide that."

She seemed to reflect, lifted her shoulders slightly,
then continued. "My sister was a *maîtresse* of the high-
est order. Trained, of course, at *le Cordon Bleu* in Paris,
but specializing in American dishes."

"Forgive me, but I have never been able to afford to
eat at the Inn on Nashua Street and so did not—"

She interrupted distractedly. "You must be my
guest some day . . . Not that the meal will be . . . Even
though Marcel is to some degree . . ." Finishing sen-
tences seemed to be a problem for her.

"And Marcel is—?" I asked.

"Jewel's *sous-chef.* He's been with her forever, but
lacks the . . . the magic, the . . ."

"Soo chef?" I said uncertainly.

"For heaven's sakes! Under-chef, second cook.
What-have-you."

What have I, indeed, I thought, besides a peppery-
tempered client? Deciding allowances must be made

for grief, I did not respond as I might have wished. Besides, I wanted very much to get the job.

She remained silent for several minutes, sipping the by now cool tea. The plate of shortbread biscuits remained untouched.

She burst into speech again. "Oh, oh, oh! It is shattering; it breaks my heart. Tragic enough to lose her dear *presence.* But without Jewel in the kitchen, things are going poorly for me. I myself am scarcely up to warming leftovers, and although Marcel is above average . . ."

She frowned, appearing to think that over. "I *believe* I can say that of Marcel, but no one can take . . . could ever take . . . the place of Jewel in the kitchen. My guests are being kind, but that won't go on forever." She leaned back, a paw to her forehead. "I fear I am ruined."

"Let us not despair," I said bracingly.

"*Yet,* you mean." There was definitely a snarl in that soft voice.

Realizing that if I were to get this job, I'd have to overlook her brusque, to say the least, manner of speech, I asked for the names of her guests and recorded them in my ledger. There were three who resided at the Inn, and several transients who had stayed overnight of late.

I rose, saying I wished to visit the Inn myself to examine the premises.

"You may ride with me in my cab," she said. "I have it waiting downstairs."

Off we went.

5

Still Not Too Savory

The Inn on Nashua Street is a large Federal-style house, almost a mansion, that has been in the Ramsey family for over a century. It has brown clapboard siding, blue trim, four gables, casement windows, and seven chimneys. The gardens are famous, and there is a stand of magnificent copper beeches, as well as a fruit orchard extending behind the house itself.

It is a handsome edifice that bespeaks decades of ladies playing croquet on the lawn, gentlemen smoking cigars in the parlor, lawyers reading wills in the library.

Alighting from the carriage, I stepped through the gate in the picket fence. Miss Clara was with the driver, asking him to wait for me, so she did not notice Conrad, the goose, come charging out of a grape arbor. Wings wide, neck extended, he raced toward me, hissing like a serpent. I would have given much at that moment if Miss Amelia Bloomer's trouser outfit for ladies had indeed come into general use. I could have vaulted the fence.

As it was, I could only shriek for Miss Clara, who turned and shouted, "Conrad! It's a friend!" He skidded to a stop on his rump in the grass and sat weaving his head from side to side, in the manner of a cobra, and not, I think, regarding me as a friend.

"Is it safe to proceed?" I asked coldly.

"But of course! He's protective of me, that's all."

"I noted that tendency in him. Did you not say his duties were only at night?"

"Since Jewel . . . since my poor sister's death . . ." She drew a deep breath. "Since then, we let him loose in the daytime, too. All manner of rowdy boys come prowling and gawking, trying to invade the grounds. It is . . . oh, it is just *awful.* So awful."

She closed her eyes, opened them, blinking. "Conrad discourages trespassers."

"I can see that he would."

She had reason to want all possible protection, and clearly the goose was ready to give his all.

"He must be a comfort," I conceded.

We went along the brick herringbone-patterned walk, up wide steps, across a pillared veranda lined with wicker chairs and tables and great jardinieres, from which spilled red and white ivy geraniums.

As we entered the Inn, a noble grandfather clock at the end of the hall deeply chimed the hour. Persian rugs lay upon the parquet floor, and a graceful curving staircase led upward to bedrooms that I doubted not would be exquisitely furnished and scented with lavender.

It was that kind of house.

To the left was a spacious drawing room, and beyond that the library. At the right was the parlor where Jewel had been found. I stepped in briefly and looked about. Beautiful chintz-covered chairs and sofa, glossy piecrust tables, a hearth with birch logs on Hessian firedogs, Staffordshire figures on the carved mantel. All in all, a delightful room.

The floor was bare, and I did not ask why.

"I wish to see the kitchen," I said, and followed her along the hall, around a corner, through swinging green baize doors.

It was completely modern, with all the latest in cooking equipment. Unlike the rest of the elegantly furnished house, the kitchen displayed no needless comfort. It was a place sternly devoted to the gastronomic arts.

"This is Marcel," said Miss Clara, indicating a tall cat standing at the huge cast-iron and nickel stove. He wore a white chef's hat and was peering critically into a pot, holding aloft a long-handled wooden spoon.

"He is, or was, Jewel's *sous-chef*," Miss Clara explained, her mouth turning down. "He is trying to take over for her. We hope he'll prove up to the task."

She certainly had a way of making ungracious remarks, *perhaps* without design. Lowering her voice slightly, she continued, "He's a manx from Quebec, and quarrelsome. I think the lack of a tail has cost him his serenity."

For my part, I was thinking that tail or no tail, this manx had a distinguished air. There was *something* about him I could not quite place. Perhaps because his all-white, enveloping chef's outfit blurred my recall?

I had no time to puzzle it out, as he burst into speech, rapid and interlaced with French.

"Jamais," he exclaimed. *"Never* do I aspire to take over for Madame Jewel! Such a coming-about is not to be thought of! *Mais, zut alors!* If only I 'ad those receipts!"

Dropping the spoon, he picked up a two-tined fork and waved it in the air. "If I 'ad those receipts! Ah, then, per'aps, I could make a going-on of this job. But all, all are gone! I am up *la* creek without a ladle!"

"Please tell me in detail about this cookery book," I said to Miss Clara.

"It's an old, old notebook containing Jewel's special recipes, which Marcel *will* call receipts, very old fashioned, but then he is . . ." She paused, as if losing her thought, then said, "Oh yes, plus a lot of Mother's and Grandmother's receipts. Recipes, I mean. We are lost without it. Marcel is a good enough under-chef. But oh dear, oh dear! Jewel's *gingerbread,* for instance. Only *she* had the touch . . ."

"Madame Jewel," Marcel began, "served 'er gingerbread warm, smothered in the clotted *crème—*"

"No one else can *begin* to duplicate it," Miss Clara broke in. "And her apricot butterscotch sticky buns! People said they were worth getting up in the morning for." She turned to Marcel. "Tell Miss . . . ah . . . Miss O'Kelly . . . about Madame Jewel's jambalaya . . ."

"Ah, *oui. Formidable.* A dish from—"

"It was an old New Orleans preparation," Miss Clara said impatiently. "Our mother came across it when she was there in '54."

"Could you not ask your mother?" I inquired. "Perhaps she would be able—"

"Mother is no longer meowing among us," Miss Clara cried out, sinking into the only chair in the kitchen, an uncomfortable-looking ladder back. "Mother gone, Jewel gone. Oh, it is beyond my strength to endure!"

"I'm so sorry," I said, rebuking myself for lack of tact. If you don't take care, I told myself severely, you'll lose this case before you get it. And you do not want to lose it.

"My sister," said the distraught Miss Clara, "took that jambalaya receipt . . . Now, you see? He has me doing it! She took that *recipe* apart and put it back together in an . . . an inimitable way. Inimitable. Mother was a fine cook, but Jewel was the star of our culinary firmament!"

"*L'étoile!*" Marcel echoed, waving his fork.

"Jewel's creations are what people expect of us," said Miss Clara. She looked sourly at Marcel. "His jambalaya is adequate, but not to be mistaken for—"

"*Je sais!*" Marcel exclaimed. "Mine is a tasty jambalaya, but Madame Jewel's was fit for Lucullus 'imself!" From his fingertips, he tossed a kiss in the air.

"Above all . . . ," Miss Clara began, wriggling in the ladder back chair and starting to sob again, "above all, if we can no longer serve Jewel's Oyster Puff, we might as well close the kitchen! That would mean closing the Inn itself!"

"*La grande Puffe!*" Marcel exclaimed. "An entrée for kings and potentates. For pharaohs and emperors!"

I was impressed. "You can't copy it?" I asked.

"*Mon Dieu!* I—I am merely a cook. Madame Jewel was an *artiste*. She was Renoir at the range! I am the copyist of the master, that is all."

"Oh, tut," Miss Clara said wearily. "Stop fishing, Marcel. We both know you are more than a copyist." Forgetting, perhaps, that a few moments earlier she'd said his cooking was only adequate.

Marcel groaned. "I tell myself it's *simplement* the matter of oysters—plump, fresh, sweet oysters—and *crème* and butter and crackers and 'erbs. *C'est tout!* That's all! But no matter 'ow I mix the mixture, it will not come out to *la Puffe magnifique* that drew diners from all corners of New England, and beyond and beyond . . ."

"There was one guest," Miss Clara murmured with a faint smile, "who said he would like to find a little door at the side of Jewel's Oyster Puff and just move in, because it was as close to heaven as a cat could come on earth."

"Fancy that!" I said weakly.

It was getting late, I was tired, all this talk of food had made me hungry, and it did not appear I was going to be offered a bite. Marcel was too busy with dinner preparations, and Miss Clara was clearly not interested in food at all.

"I shall go home now," I informed her, "and plan my approach. Ah—I see your policeman has arrived. You'll be quite safe, between him and Conrad."

Stationed at the gate, where the cab was waiting to take me back to my office, was a blue-uniformed figure. He turned at my approach, started back elaborately, lifted his helmet slightly, and said, "Well, cross me heart and hope to make sergeant before I die, if it isn't Eileen O'Kelly, Boston's very own lady gumshoe!"

"Good evening, Shane Finley," I said. "I hope I find you unwell."

I climbed into the cab and indicated to the driver that I was ready to leave.

"Walk on," he said to his horse, lifting the reins and letting them fall gently on the broad brown back.

That night I sat up late, devising an approach to the problem, and in the early hours of the morning arrived at what seemed to me a place to begin looking for Madame Jewel's killer.

Case pending

6

The Suspect Husband

Clara Ramsey's case was truly desperate, and I was working hard on it. Yet other jobs were coming my way, and as I had to pay rent on the office and my room, and put food on the table, I was obliged to accept some of them.

One day there came to my office, like a duchess ducking into a saloon, none other than Mrs. Avery Johnstone III, her very own High Society Siamese self.

I indicated a visitor's chair, and she sat, tucking her silken skirts close, draping her slender brown tail across her lap, as if to avoid contact with my furniture.

After a moment's silence she explained—an explanation for her presence in such a place obviously necessary—that she had noticed the sign on my door some months before, when Madame Zorina had had her establishment here. As I had anticipated, my friend Bertha had indeed moved on to finer quarters.

"Not that then I could have dreamed—" My elegant visitor broke off with a vexed air, then continued in a rush, "Be that as it may, here I am."

In an effort to put her at ease, I inquired about Bertha. "I understand Madame Zorina is doing well," I said, glancing at my client's veiled and beflowered pale yellow straw hat. She wore a suit of daffodil yellow shantung with brown silk braiding, glacé kid gloves, and an opal stud in her left ear. Her ruffled brown silk parasol had a lacy gold handle. A delicate, pricey scent hovered about her.

She did not answer my observation, declining, I suppose, to discuss a milliner with a detective.

I offered tea.

With an assessing glance at my tea wagon, she nodded stiffly, and I busied myself with preparations, thinking that probably her service was silver and made by Paul Revere.

Keeping her gloves on, she lifted her veil, took a sip of tea, and scrutinized my face carefully.

At length she said, "I think—that is, I want—I wish to have my—to have you follow—that is, to find out something about—about—"

Her voice was so low that I practically had to crawl over my desk to hear what she was trying to tell me.

"Yes?" I said in soothing, ladylike tones. "Perhaps I may be of help?"

A dainty cough behind a gloved hand. Then, "My *husband*," she gasped. "I want you to—to follow him. I don't know the word for that—activity," she added with upper-class distaste for lower-class terms.

"Tail."

"Tail?"

"The word for the—activity—is *tail*."

"How droll," she said. *How vulgar,* she meant.

"If you wish the etymology," said I, making clear that fluency of phrase was not beyond me, "it simply means that I stay on a subject as closely and quietly as his—or her—own tail."

"How demeaning for you." She took another sip of tea, waiting, I thought, for me to justify my demeaning occupation.

I remained mute.

She put her cup on the desk and looked at my window boxes. "Your flowers are pretty," she said.

"I like them."

"You have a pleasant view."

"I look at it a lot."

If she took all morning, I would wait until she stated the problem, one I'd already surmised.

"Oh dear, oh dear. This is so difficult."

"Perhaps, then, you should wait? Until it does not seem so difficult?"

"No, no! I must be sure. I *must.* One way or the other, I have to know! That is—I must find out. I cannot sleep for not knowing—" When a cat can't sleep, the situation is urgent. Still, I waited for her to go on.

With a trembling breath, she said, "Miss O'Kelly, I come to you because—because I have reason to believe that my husband is—ah, that he is—oh, dear—I believe he may be *second-timing* me. Have I phrased it correctly?"

"'Two-timing' is more usual."

"You should know," she said with a faint sniff and pushed a photograph toward me. "Here is a likeness of him. Taken in one of Boston's finest photographic studios."

Where else?

It showed a distinguished gentleman Siamese, very much arrayed. Dark frock coat, striped pants, pale spats, watch chain with fob, sweeping whiskers. A silk topper perched on a pedestal beside him. And—in no way to be disguised—a glint in his slanted eyes that said second-timing was first nature to him.

"Is not he the handsomest man you ever saw?" she all but gushed.

I looked up in surprise and saw that she did, indeed, expect an admission of her husband's fine personal appearance.

"Good-looking," I agreed.

Another silence ensued, and then I said, "If you are quite sure—"

"I am," she said miserably. "I ask you to find the truth for me. I *must* have the truth, no matter what it is."

I agreed to tail a gentleman I was already sure was a cat about town in a very big way. She did not protest when I named my fee and asked for an advance, simply took some crisp bills from her beaded handbag and put them on the desk, on her side, so that I would have been obliged to reach.

I left them there.

With reluctance she gave me the name of his exceedingly exclusive club, and the hours when I would be likely to find him there.

She departed, back straight, saying she would come by in a week to see what I had—she choked on the words— what I had found out.

Throughout our interview she had avoided my eyes, kept her gloves on, and had patently found everything about me, my

office, her reason for being in it, distressing and distasteful. But I reached across my desk for the lovely green bills without a quiver of shame.

I will *not* be condescended to.

That afternoon, I rode my bicycle across town through a faint drizzle and waited outside his club. I was wearing my usual tailing disguise—a reversible beret pulled down on my ears, pink on one side, blue on the other, and a reversible cape, same colors. I switch around when on a subject, thus altering my appearance. In this instance, I reasoned that a gent like this would more quickly spy a bug crossing his path than notice a female who looked like me.

I was, of course, correct in my estimate of the

upper-class clubman. When he emerged from the great, carved, oaken front door, held open for him by a liveried servant, he stood on the steps for a few moments, eyes going right, left, and over my head. Lifting his gold-knobbed Malacca stick, he hailed a passing cab. I had no doubt that a carriage with matched pair was stabled at his home, but for certain activities public conveyance is more convenient.

Climbing in, he directed the coachman, and off went the hack, with Eileen O'Kelly pedaling after.

Needless to say, it did not take a week to discover that he was not two-timing her, and I said this when she next came to the office.

"He is not?" she said. "He *isn't?*" She looked into my eyes for the first time. "You are telling me the real *truth?*"

I felt like saying I don't deal in unreal truths and even, for a fleeting moment, considered leaving her under the impression that she had a faithful spouse. It would be the easiest course, even factual, to report that he was not two-timing her, because he wasn't.

At the very least, he was twenty-timing her.

But there was my professional pride to consider, my ethics as a trustworthy investigator. Clearing my throat, I said, "It is true that he is not—as it is put—two-timing you . . ."

"What exactly are you saying? Explain yourself, Miss O'Kelly! I will not have evasions from an employee!"

"Very well." I sighed. "Your husband is not seeing one other cat. He is seeing a variety of them, all over Boston and Cambridge. And in Ipswich."

She sat for a long moment, looking at my window boxes, then rose. "I have friends in Ipswich, *Miss*

O'Kelly. I have not the faintest doubt that they would have let me know if your imputation had merit. The only conclusion is that you could not do your job and have taken my money under false pretenses."

I rose in turn. "If that is how you feel," I said, weary of her and her problem and her husband, "I shall return the fee in full."

"Keep it! Just remember—I can make trouble if you dare ever utter a *word* of these—insinuations."

"In this office, a client's report is completely confidential—," I began, unable to keep my voice from shaking, whether from rage or humiliation I am still uncertain.

But Mrs. Avery Johnstone III, who, after all, had wanted the truth only if it was unreal, swept from my office, still holding her skirts close, avoiding contamination.

Case concluded

ADDENDUM: That's the last *time I accept an undertaking of this kind.*

7

The
Catnip-Nabbing

After washing my paws of Mrs. Avery Johnstone III, I undertook a case of industrial espionage, going undercover at Faire's Flora in Sudbury. This is a large, generations-old family company where domestic and exotic herbs and other plants are grown and shipped locally and around the world.

It appeared that one of the employees was selling secrets to a rival firm that was planning to bring out a line of cat cosmetics scented with the queen of herbs: CATNIP.

Faire's Flora grows the world's best 'nip, and Mr. Groveland, the present owner, great-grandson of the founder, had already decided to go into the cosmetics business himself. When he discovered, to his horror, that a competitor had got hold of some of his finest plants, he came rushing to me.

"You can see," he told me, stroking his long whiskers with a slightly unsteady paw, wrinkling his brow, "that this traitor in my employ must be uncovered quickly, or the competition will duplicate my formula. Using my own catnip! Think of it!"

The thought of the outrage was making him so tense that he became flat-eared and bristle-furred. It was not nice to think how, when and if I discovered the culprit, said culprit would be dealt with. For a moment I hesitated even to take the job.

"If you are asking yourself," he went on, "why I got in touch with you, a female spy—"

"Please," I protested. "Detective. Or investigator. *Not* spy."

"Be that as it may. I come to you instead of to a regular detective because I have only women working in the greenhouses."

"I'll do my best, of course," I said coldly, vexed by his explanation, since I had not wondered at all why he had decided upon my services. I am a good investigator, and my reputation is growing. That is sufficient reason to consult me.

"I am proud to say, in perfect truth," he was going on in an edgy, irritable tone, "that I have always had a fine—a very very good—relationship with my workers, male and female. So it is doubly dismaying to find myself betrayed. I pay good wages, give regular rest periods during the day, which is more than the average businessman is prepared to do—"

He was right in that. Most businessmen resent as slackers employees who take time out to stretch briefly. Giving them regular rest periods was, in my experience, unheard of. I looked at Mr. Groveland more appreciatively. A self-important windbag in one way, but a kindly one. I assured him I would do my very best to see that his formula was not purloined.

When, on the following day, I arrived at Faire's

Flora and was conducted to one of the long green-houses where basil, rosemary, parsley, lemon grass, sage, thyme, verbena, and that finest of herbs—catnip—were grown, I was gowned in a green smock and given a double gauze mask to protect against the heady, aromatic scents. Especially that of the 'nip.

Even so, that especial scent was heavy on the air.

The head gardener had instructed me to keep my mask on and breathe through my mouth in order to keep from suddenly rolling on the floor in ecstasy.

"We tell all our workers to wear the masks and breathe through their mouths, but we can't go around all day checking to see if everyone's sniffing on the up and up, can we?"

"I grant that would not be practical. But you must have quite an employee turnover," I said as he was lowering cotton blinds against the sun.

"You have no idea the trouble we see. We give regular ten-minute periods out in the fresh air every two hours. And we rotate workers from one department to another on a weekly basis. Take them out of herbs and put them into scentless vines or shrubs. But inevitably some cats get hooked, and we have to let them go. Sad, but we must be firm."

Well! I had no intention of starting on the downward path to catnip addiction, so from then on I wore a *triple* mask and breathed heavily through my mouth eight hours a day, except at lunchtime, and during my ten-minute rest periods every two hours. This continued for nearly two weeks.

It took me that long to uncover the industrial spy, and then by accident, though of course I didn't tell that to Mr. Groveland.

One morning as I was repotting mint and lemon basil, I happened to glance at a worker well down the line from me, who was transferring shoots from small to larger pots. We were all doing that, and it was work so boring that after a while one's eyes glazed over. This is probably why, I am ashamed to admit, it took me so long to find her. She was a skinny little thing, so small that I hadn't noticed her before. All the employees except me were yawning and swaying blearily over the job in hand. As I looked up to give my eyes a rest, I observed this little marmalade tabby slip a shoot of catnip into her smock pocket.

I'll give her this, she was deft as a dip.

(Dip: *pickpocket,* for those who don't know the lingo.)

Watching stealthily, I saw that about every fourth shootling went not into a pot but a pocket. I continued with the tedious transferals until just before the shift was over. Then I went to Mr. Groveland with my discovery. I was not proud of myself, unmasking a puny, bony little cat like that. Some of my jobs are nothing to purr over. But there, it is my chosen profession, and I must take the bitter with the better.

Mr. Groveland, his security chief, and I crouched behind a stand of yew until the workers came out on their way home.

My suspect was the last to leave. She was met by a scruffy, shifty-eyed party straight from the alley, who took to his paws as we closed in on them, leaving the little thief frightened and defenseless, her pockets stuffed with first-grade catnip.

She began to yowl, and I felt like yowling along with her.

It turned out that she had a litter of six kittens to support and had been unable to resist, when it was offered, this method of earning extra money to feed and house them.

Mr. Groveland, a soft-hearted businessman if ever there was one, not only didn't fire her, he raised her salary, on condition she work only in vines and shrubs from then on, and promise to go straight in the future.

I am sure she will.

Despite the nature of my work, I still tend to think the best of cats.

Sometime later, Mr. Groveland sent me a flacon of his first creation, which he calls:

FORGET THE PAST
A FRAGRANCE FOR FELINES

It was a nice thought, though I do not wear scents myself. How could I tail a suspect while trailing catnip perfume like a broken bottle?

Case concluded

53

8

The
Tearaway Teen

Miss Clara Ramsey had come to me in early August, a month with no *R* in it. Oysters are only to be eaten in months containing the letter *R*. My plan was to discover, by whatever means, the whereabouts of a restaurant offering, during months enriched by this letter, an oyster dish of rare quality. It seemed a slim hope, but I could not at the time come up with a better idea.

Meanwhile, there was an alternative I could undertake immediately. Like all cats, I have a shocking number of relatives. My immediate and extended family is to be found the length and breadth of New England and neighboring states. Again, like all cats, I don't keep in touch much with my relatives. But the present matter required extraordinary effort.

I got word to all those cats I could think of, asking that they in turn spread word among their friends and relations that a reward would be paid for information leading to the discovery of anyone offering an oyster dish of rare quality . . .

While awaiting word from them—none came—and waiting for August to turn to September, bringing with it the letter *R*, I continued to take on other jobs.

One morning as I was sorting through my files, there was a knock on the door.

"Come in," I called.

A pair of striped tabbies entered my office. It is not unheard of, but is unusual, for two clients to consult me at once. I invited them to sit, offered tea, which was refused, and asked what I could do for them.

Without giving names, they plunged immediately into their unhappy tale, taking turns to speak.

"We want you to find our daughter," said the wife.

"Tosca. Her name is Tosca," said the husband.

"Named for the opera, you know."

"We are opera lovers."

"Especially Italian opera."

Italian opera, any sort of opera, was one of the many areas of culture of which I was ignorant. Why is it, I asked myself, that I never have time for anything but work?

Musing thus, I lost track of what this couple was saying and grasped at the only word I recalled.

"Your daughter's name is Tosca," I said, trying to project an air of competence.

"Named for the opera," the wife repeated.

"We have season tickets," said the husband.

"To the opera," I said, as if making a point.

"Yes, yes. To the opera," said she.

"That does not mean we have much money," said he.

"For the season tickets, we are happy to go without other things."

"But that does not mean that we are unwilling to pay your fee."

"Or unable."

"Certainly not unable."

Thinking it time to get down to cases, I said, "You do not know where Tosca is? That is the—difficulty?"

"Yes. No, we do not know where she is," said the wife.

"How long has she been—when did you last see her?"

"Three days ago," said the husband.

"It is—we are unable to—we have always kept the closest eye upon her."

"Always. We protect her."

I could see they were repressing anguish with difficulty, yet were determined to repress it.

"Would you care to give me your names?" I asked.

"Yes. Of course," he said and fell silent.

I waited. Patience is a virtue, and certainly one of mine.

"We are Mr. and Mrs. Vivaldi," she admitted at last.

They eyed me as if expecting a reaction. Should I know the name? Know them? They looked an undistinguished pair, but were perhaps prominent in circles of which I knew nothing? Possibly for "undistinguished" I should substitute "modest"?

"We do not claim descent from the great violinist and composer," said the husband.

"Ah," said I, not pretending knowledge of whom he spoke, but again struck with how little I knew aside from my daily routine. This is a matter that must be corrected, I decided. As the saying goes, "All work and no play makes Puss a dull girl."

"Well, Mr. and Mrs. Vivaldi," I said briskly, opening the small notebook I carry when in the field. "I shall need particulars."

"Particulars?"

I can't recall which of them said that. Their voices blended so, and getting anything pertinent from either was exceedingly difficult.

"Information about your daughter's activities," I explained. "Who her friends are, what her interests are. I need to know something *about* her."

"Her *friends*—," Mr. Vivaldi began, "call her—" He put a paw to his face, as though with toothache. "Call her—"

"They call her *Tossy*," Mrs. Vivaldi offered dispiritedly.

"Most children have nicknames," I said. "I used to be called Leeny."

"Tosca doesn't like her beautiful name. She *asks* people to call her—Tossy." Mr. Vivaldi's eyes narrowed with what appeared to me actual anger. Surely an exaggerated reaction?

"Well," I said, "if you will give me the names of some of her friends, that would be a place for me to start."

Silence.

"She does have friends? Girls and boys she sees outside of school?"

"No boys!" he snapped. "She goes to a girls' school."

"At church, then."

"No!"

"But she does have girlfriends?"

"She is allowed to invite a couple of girls home, after school. Sometimes. Now and then." That was Mrs. Vivaldi speaking. She added, "They seem—all right."

Silence again.

"If you would give me names?" I was almost pleading.

"Of these girls, you mean? The ones who sometimes come to the house?"

"Yes. Please. Those, and any others you can think of."

Mrs. Vivaldi pondered a moment. "There's Emma?" She looked at her husband for confirmation.

He nodded.

"And Anna. She's part Burmese. Something of a snob about it."

"What are their last names?" I asked.

They exchanged nervous glances.

"I don't think she told us," Mrs. Vivaldi said, in a voice so low I could scarcely hear.

"Perhaps she did, but we don't recall—"

"That Anna," Mrs. Vivaldi said hesitantly. "The Burmese. Her last name is Chang, I think. Or Chung. Something like that."

"Who cares about their names—," the husband burst out. "She's not with girls! It's those awful boys, those teenage tomcats who are always hanging around, trying to get a glimpse of her!"

"Tosca is very pretty," said Mrs. Vivaldi.

"Tosca is *beautiful,*" he corrected.

"Naturally, she attracts—attention."

"That would be all right, in the proper circumstances."

"And what would those be?" I asked.

"Have I not just told you?" he all but shouted. "It's those tomcats! That's what has us frightened out of our fur."

"I suppose Tosca does not ask any of them in?"

A gasp from Mrs. Vivaldi. "Boys? Ask boys to come in our *house?* In our home!"

Unable to speak, Mr. Vivaldi growled. Snarled would not be putting it too strongly.

"Girls. We only permit her to associate with girls," said his wife. She turned her head from side to side, as if sniffing danger. "Emma. Anna. Tosca once mentioned another girl, but not her name."

"We know nothing about this other girl."

That appeared to make three girls Tosca might have for friends, none of whom the parents knew well enough to remember their last names. I thought of the many girlfriends of my own teenagery, remembered how we used to gang together, go roller-skating together, go in a group to ice-cream parlors where we devoured hot-fudge sundaes, to Saturday night, strictly chaperoned dances. As we went to all-girl schools, that was the only time we saw boys, except at church. I recalled our girls' overnights at one another's homes, remembered how we'd go down to the kitchen in our nightgowns and make cocoa. How we giggled and gossiped and carried on—in total innocence.

"Does Tosca spend a night now and then with one of her girlfriends?"

"No, no, no!" Mr. Vivaldi exclaimed excitedly. "*That* we never permit. Think what could happen—what such imprudence might lead to. No! Such a thing is out of the question."

So, I said to myself. They don't trust Tosca. They fear what they can't put a name to.

Nonetheless, I understood what they meant about teenage tomcats. Granted, individuals among cats that age can be all right, lots of them doubtlessly nice, decent fellows. Even two together is not especially alarming. But when I see three or more coming toward me, I cross to the other side of the street. A pair of youths might be friends strolling together. More than two is a gang.

That part of this couple's anxiety I could sympathize with. I guessed that they were in terror lest Tosca had eloped with one of the forbidden boys. It was a thought they could not possibly express, even to a detective whose help they were seeking.

I was beginning to think that Tosca had simply gone to find a place where she could breathe without instruction, without four frantically loving eyes watching her every move.

I thought she'd probably come home on her own in a few days.

"Well!" I pushed my chair back. "I should like, with your permission, to see Tosca's room."

"Why?"

"Must you?"

Irritation was beginning to tickle my throat. "Unless I can form a picture of your daughter's surroundings—"

"Here!" he broke in, producing a Manila envelope he'd been holding. "Here are pictures—"

He leaned across the desk to hand me half a dozen poses, studio-taken, of the elusive Tosca. She was certainly a most beautiful young creature, mostly silver, with black stripes.

I prevented myself from glancing at their wholly undistinguished selves, but wondered how in the world they had produced this radiant kitty with the flower-like face. I began to understand their unbalanced pride in a child that must seem, to them, a miracle.

I rose. "We will go now," I said in a firm voice.

We rode by trolley to a street just over in Cambridge. It was by no means a shabby neighborhood. Just drab.

A cursory inspection of Tosca's room revealed little. A normal teenager's room. Very untidy. Long-legged dolls on the bed. Books. I examined some of these. Mrs. Radcliffe, Miss Alcott, the Brontës, Mrs. Gaskell. All women writers, I noticed. Perhaps she was not permitted daring male writers. Henry Adams, for instance. Or William Dean Howells. There was nothing about music.

"Does Tosca share your love of opera?" I asked.

"She does not—," Mr. Vivaldi began, but was unable to continue.

"No," his wife said. "She refuses to go with us." After a moment she said, as if confessing a shameful fact, "Tosca likes this modern sort of—of *music*. Ragtime. The jazz." She shook her head in bafflement.

I am, myself, a devotee of jazz and ragtime, but of course said nothing. I glanced briefly at the parlor. A baby grand piano nearly filled it, with many musical scores in a case nearby. A gramophone with a great tulip-shaped horn stood in the corner, a neat stack of records in a bookcase beside it. I didn't have to look to know that there'd be no Louis Moreau Gottschalk or Scott Joplin or W. C. Handy represented.

Three of my favorite music men. And, probably, of Tosca's.

Consulting the Cambridge directory, I found no Changs, but there was a family named Chung whose address was close to that of the Vivaldis'.

Making my way there, I mounted the steps of a brownstone house. Music was coming out of the window. It sounded like a player piano.

I rang the bell, and a nice-looking, plump, brown lady answered.

"Mrs. Chung?" I inquired.

"That's me."

"I am Eileen O'Kelly. A private investigator."

"Mercy. What are you doing here?"

"I have been asked by the parents of Tosca Vivaldi to—to find her. Do you know her? Is she a friend of your daughter's?"

"Of course we know Tossy. She's right here."

"Her parents don't know that. They haven't heard from her in three days. They are frightened and frantic."

"Come in, come in," she said quickly. "This is most puzzling. Tossy said her father and mother knew she was coming for the weekend. It's the first time it's ever happened, but she did say—"

"I see. Well, they don't know it. They don't know where she is."

"Mercy. How upsetting for them. For me, too. I

don't like being lied to. She doesn't seem the sort of girl who would tell, well, fibs. Oh my goodness, what a shock. Come along, do. The girls are in the parlor. This way, Miss Kelly."

Not bothering to correct her, I followed her down the hall to a large room where a group of girls was gathered round the player piano. The large punctuated cylinder was turning, and a girl on the bench pedaled away, pretending to tickle the ivories.

They were all, including Tosca, who stood out as the prettiest, singing loudly and happily about a bird in a gilded cage who had everything to make her happy. But how could a bird, or a girl, be happy in a cage, even though it was made of gold?

When they'd finished the song, they burst out

laughing and looked at Tosca, who shrugged her slim shoulders and smiled shyly.

"Tossy," said Mrs. Chung, "there is a lady here to see you. To take you home, dear. Your parents are worried about you."

Tosca turned, started to protest, then sighed and followed me out of the room, waving good-bye to the other girls without looking back.

She ducked her head as she passed Mrs. Chung and mumbled, "I'm sorry." There were tears in her eyes.

"I'm sorry, too," said Mrs. Chung. I admired her for not telling Tosca she certainly *should* be sorry.

Outside we walked for a while in silence, before Tosca spoke. "I know you think I'm horrible."

"No, I don't think that. I think you feel overprotected."

"I feel *caged*. Like it says in the song. A bird in a cage. You saw how they all looked at me. They know I'm practically a prisoner."

"Your parents love you very much."

"I know they do. I wish they didn't. Anyway, not so much. Not the *way* they love me."

It was not my place to lecture her, but neither could I say how well I understood her feelings. It would be a betrayal of her parents, my clients, who were sick with fear for her.

"Perhaps if you all three had a talk together—," I began.

"I've tried that."

"Perhaps you should try again. Perhaps this—escapade—has alarmed them enough so they'd be willing to hear your side. They really are very very frightened."

She didn't answer or speak again until we got her home.

Well!

As it says in novels, "Reader, I draw a veil over the ensuing scene."

I draw one because it was so full of emotion and recrimination and noisy talk and tears that I didn't stay for it. I ran down the stoop and caught the next trolley back to Boston.

The following day, Mr. Vivaldi came to the office to pay my fee.

"We cannot—cannot possibly thank you enough," he said, his voice shaking.

"It was my job." I could not resist adding, "I hope that matters are . . . that things are working out for you and Mrs. Vivaldi and Tosca."

"Tosca has agreed never to do such a wicked thing again. Frightening us half to death. No. It will not happen again."

"I see."

So much for hearing Tosca's side.

Handing me an envelope, he left before I could open it.

Within was the amount I'd specified as my fee. There was a scribbled note from Mrs. Vivaldi, saying that they were going to try to work things out with their daughter and thanking me again for my diligence in finding her.

I wondered whether Mr. and Mrs. Vivaldi were going to see eye to eye about this problem, and I was certainly glad that it was none of mine.

Also included were two tickets to an opera.

Tosca.

I'd never been to an opera, but decided that if Bertha would go with me, it might be a start toward having something in my life besides work. It would also give me a chance to have a night out with my old friend, whom I had not seen in ages.

It seemed about time for both.

Case concluded

9

In Perfect Truth

Although it had appeared a likely approach, my plan to discover through my network of friends and relations the existence of a superior oyster dish being served somewhere in New England did not produce results. September came, passed, October arrived, with not a whisper from any quarter of an extraordinary oyster dish being served anywhere in New England.

I was getting discouraged.

On a hazy morning in late October, I was sitting in my office, gazing at the familiar field. Among tall weeds and browning grass, late blue asters were blooming. Between the field and the woods beyond, a low stone wall, crumbling in places, was covered with orange bittersweet and purple chokecherry. Beyond the wall, the woods were aflame with the brilliance of dying leaves.

There I sat, wondering if I would ever have anything in my life besides work. I hadn't, as I'd once planned, gone to any of Boston's fine museums, its famous public library. I had not visited Mrs. Jack Gardner's well-known collection of paintings and *objets d'art*. I'd not asked Bertha to go to the opera with me. *Tosca* wasn't scheduled to be performed until after Christmas, but still—I could have asked her. Maybe I had unconsciously decided not to go at all? What would I wear? The thought of actually going to an opera intimidated me, not a person easily intimidated. Band concerts on Sunday in the park, that was my kind of music.

I told myself I was too busy for culture. Smokey Jack was in Cuba playing winter ball, and I hadn't heard from

Miss Clara in a fortnight, but I had a number of jobs on hand—none, I think, sufficiently interesting to record.

Then, on a dreary day in November, Miss Clara arrived at my office looking at once teary-eyed and determined.

"It is impossible to continue," she said. "I am getting short of guests, short of money, short of . . ."

"Of patience?"

"No!" she said shrilly. "Can you not understand why I've lost heart? Are you unable, Miss O'Kelly, to comprehend such a simple truth? Doubtless it is not your fault—" She paused to make clear that it was, indeed and doubtless, my fault "—that you are unable to accomplish what you undertook to do, which the police can't do either, but I am obliged to accept that we shall never know who murdered my darling Jewel and stole her notebook of receipts. Recipes," she amended angrily.

"The Inn," I said, delicately picking my way, "is—ah—still open, I know."

"A wraith of what it was. No longer do we take reservations months in advance, nor turn away guests who lack them. *Au contraire!* as Marcel would put it. We all but snatch people off the street and beg them to accept our hospitality. At reduced rates."

She shuddered, fell briefly silent, then continued. "No, no, no . . . it is not the Inn on Nashua Street that once it was. Marcel is competent, but cannot revive past culinary glories."

"How *is* Marcel?"

"Exhausted. We are all exhausted. Conrad is worn out chasing rowdy young tomcats who invade the grounds now that the constable they used to post at our gate is gone. He's losing his feathers."

A spiritless Conrad, losing his feathers, was sad to contemplate.

"The police," Miss Clara went on, "have given up on us altogether. *That* much is clear."

"The Boston police never give up on a murder—," I began, but was, of course, interrupted.

"So they say, but I see no signs of it. I am sorry to tell you, Miss O'Kelly, that I shall have to terminate our arrangement. If you will send your bill . . . ." She waved a paw. "I must settle with myself to lead a life without hope."

I thought she might have shown more spunk. But there! I hadn't lost a sister I loved. Nor was I in danger of losing my business. I was doing well, for a "lady gumshoe."

It was this apparently unsolvable case that robbed me of rest. Madame Jewel Ramsey's murderer was as free as he (she?) had been in early August, and I had to concede that my method of uncovering the culprit, which had seemed so promising in September, began to appear futile as the year crept to a finish.

I'd had not a single lead. Nevertheless, I convinced Miss Clara to allow me a little more time.

When, by chance, the lead came, it was from a completely unexpected source.

On a morning of face-pinching cold, I biked out wearing my winter disguise, the reversible cap and cape now woolen, to continue a watch I'd begun on a marmalade tabby suspected of embezzling from his employers, a group of accountants.

As I sped around a corner, head down, I all but ran into a portly gentleman.

Braking hard, I was tumbling to the ground, when a

stout arm held me firmly up, and a voice said, "My dear, are you all right?"

As I was clearly at fault, this civility surprised me. He looked so sleek and pleased with himself, so unlike the edgy, anxious cat I'd met months ago, that it took me a moment to recognize Mr. Groveland of Faire's Flora.

"Why, Miss O'Kelly," he said now. "I wouldn't have known you!"

My cap and cape are not flattering, but a little tact never hurts. "I'm in disguise," I snapped, then relented because a happy face is irresistible. "*You* look like—like the King of the Cats."

"How well you put it! That's just how I feel! Yes, yes, yes! Things go well, very well indeed, with me. I can say in perfect truth that things, with me, could not be better! But I observe you are not wearing *Forget the Past*."

"Wha—oh yes. No. I can't wear scent when on the job. Such a lovely fragrance would give me away immediately." Actually, I had never unstoppered the flacon, not being one for artificial aids to attraction. Let me allure on my merits, that's my motto. Not that I'd done any alluring for some time.

"Ah, but of course, I see, I see," he said heartily, his thoughts already elsewhere. That is to say, on himself. "I am sure you will be happy to hear that Miss Willow Carberry and I were married this past month!"

"Miss—Miss *Carberry?* She who—"

"The very one! I found that when the dear creature was sure she could support her little brood, she quite bloomed. Ha, ha! *Bloomed!* Appropriate for a lady wedded to the owner of Faire's Flora, would you not say? She opened—flowerlike—in the sunny air of security. In—I proudly add—the sunny air of *love.* Yes, yes—I can say, in perfect truth, that she *blossomed.*"

He was most eager for me to appreciate his play on words.

Not to disappoint, I said, "Oh, that is *so* droll, Mr. Groveland." I tried to move forward, but was held by his paw on the handlebar.

"I took her out of the greenhouses," he went on, "into my office. There we came to—to know and to love—each other. Deeply, deeply."

"Think of that," I said, again wheeling forward a little. But he was not to be stopped. Tightening his grip on the handlebar, he said purrily, "We have just returned from our honeymoon!"

I did not wish to be discourteous, so I said, "How wonderful! And where did you go, may I ask?"

"To a new, a very fine, hostelry near Baltimore, right on the Chesapeake Bay. We are fanciers of fine seafood, Mrs. Groveland and I. Ah, the pleasure it gives me to say those two exquisite words—Mrs. Groveland! You cannot imagine—"

"Seafood?" I interrupted. My whiskers quivered. The fur on my back prickled. "Does this—this hostelry—serve any *special* seafood dishes?"

"I can say in perfect truth, *all* they serve must be termed special. Excellent crab cakes. A superior crab bisque. The Chesapeake Bay is famous for its crabs, you know. And also for its—"

"Its *oysters!*" I exclaimed.

"My word!" He was a bit surprised at my reaction. "Yes, indeedy. We experienced such a taste thrill—" He frowned faintly. "Although—I did, at the time, think I had tasted just such a delicacy sometime before—"

I all but seized his lapels. "Did you have a dish called Oyster Puff?"

"It wasn't *called* that," he said thoughtfully. He straightened and said, "Oh, my word! Yes, yes. That's *it,* Miss O'Kelly! I thought, as I was eating the delicious dish, which they call—let me see, now—aha! *Oyster Bubble.* It crossed my mind, as I relished each mouthful, that this was not, in truth, the *first* time I had experienced this especial taste thrill, but I see now what you are getting at! It was, I can say in perfect truth, the equal, the *duplicate* of poor murdered Madame Jewel's renowned Oyster Puff, which I have so often savored at the Inn on Nashua Street, although not, in the past, in the company of my adorable wife—"

He began to sense that my interest in his great happiness was waning. "Tell me," he inquired, "has the felon been apprehended?"

"Not yet," I said guardedly.

Not yet, but soon perhaps, if my theory proved correct.

"How came this person in Maryland to be serving Madame Jewel's Puff?" Mr. Groveland asked.

"It's a question that I believe *you* may have found the answer to." I hesitated to mention the reward to so affluent a party, but felt obliged to say, "If what I suspect turns out to be fact, a reward has been offered—"

"Oh, *tut!*" said he. "Pshaw! Just keep me informed of developments. I can say in perfect—"

I couldn't wait while he assured me, at his usual slow pace, that he said everything in perfect truth.

"What is the name of the person running the hostelry in Maryland?" I demanded. "Do you recall the name?"

"Now, let me think. We stayed there several days. The rooms are handsome, and I, of course, took the best, an elegant suite overlooking the bay so that we could watch the activity of the fishermen. Mrs. Groveland was quite overwhel—"

"Please, Mr. Groveland. Can you recall the name of the innkeeper?"

"I'm trying to, am I not? Just give me—*Lindeman,* that was it. He and his wife call their place The Mariner and His Mate. There's a wooden sign, hand painted, swinging over the door, depicting a sailor staring out to sea through a spyglass. No sign of the mate in it, but I understand that they, too, were but recently wed—"

"Thank you, thank you, dear Mr. Groveland. Please remember me kindly to Mrs. Groveland—"

Forgetting that I'd set out to follow a possibly pilfering marmalade tabby, I pedaled off to Nashua Street.

How sadly the Inn had come down in the world!

Lawns and grounds had a seedy air, there were weeds in the border gardens, and in an indefinable way, the great beautiful house, once so resplendent, seemed dowdy.

Conrad, now lacking even rowdy boys to chase, rested dispiritedly near the steps. He declined to challenge me. The stable, where in the past the carriage trade had stabled its rigs, was empty except for one surrey, and a small bay horse tossing his feed bag to get the last of the oats.

Within, all was quiet, and no longer immaculate. The crystal chandelier was faintly dusty, the grandfather clock silent for lack of winding, the drawing room untidy, the parlor door shut. Over all an air of silent resignation that made me sad, so sad.

Going swiftly down the hall to the kitchen, I found Miss Clara and Marcel washing dishes. They had been obliged to let pot boys and kitchenmaids go.

They turned at my entrance, one glance telling them that I had, at last, something to report.

"What is it?" Miss Clara cried out. "You have something to tell me!"

"I am not *altogether* sure," I said, "but we may be making progress. I need to know the name of the guest who said he would like to find a door in the Oyster Puff and move in because it was—"

"You can't mean Mr. *Lindeman?*" she interrupted. "Mr. Frederick Lindeman, who comes here . . . that is, used to come here often, staying for a few days and . . . and spoke so fancy and was so devoted to my sister? Anyway, to her cooking. He used to say that no one else in the . . ."

She broke off and got out one of her mourning hankies, exclaiming, "It is not to be *believed.* Mr. Lindeman!"

Marcel, clasping a platter to his chest like a shield, was scowling horribly.

I said, "When I asked for a list of your guests, you did not include this Mr. Lindeman's name. Why not?"

"I . . . it never crossed my mind that he . . ." She put a paw to her mouth. "Why, it is true! He has not been back since . . . since . . ."

"Tell me—did he ever order anything except the Puff?"

"Never. Sometimes he would have two. He savored them, more than anyone else did, even though everyone else, of course, also said they had never tasted . . ." She stumbled to the ladder back chair. "You actually think that Mr. *Lindeman* . . ."

"*Sans doute,* 'e was attempting to commit the dish to memory!" That from Marcel.

"One thing more," I said. "Did he ever meet, or even see, Marcel?

"But no! Marcel remained always in the kitchen.

The *sous-chef* is not called to the dining room to receive congratulations."

I glanced at the *sous-chef,* now chef *sans "sous."* Placing the platter on a sideboard, he had seized a carving knife and begun charging around the room.

"Villain!" he shouted. "Scoundrel! I will kill 'im to pieces! 'E did to the death she who was a *chef magnifique.* Let me at 'im! Where is this thieving, killing scoundrel to be found? Tell me, Mam'selle Eileen!"

"Stop that, Marcel!" Miss Clara snapped. "If you can't be helpful, then go someplace and compose yourself. Or stay here and keep quiet. I need to know what Miss O'Kelly has in her mind, not what you have in yours."

I wondered why he tolerated her barbed tongue, or, for that matter, why I did. The question seemed to answer itself. Miss Clara was his employer and my client. We had our livings to get and had dispositions able to overlook short-tempered employers.

I had a pleasing thought. Our natures, his and mine, were similar.

"D'accord!" he said, calming at once. "I will listen."

I admired him for his ardor, for his self-control, for his loyalty to this temperamental woman.

Placing the knife on a counter, he turned to me attentively.

"Tell us," he said, "what we need to know."

I realized then, that he was not, as I had thought, intimidated by Miss Clara. He was—is—indifferent to her irascibility. As must anyone be who associates with her.

I told them what I had in mind.

10

Overnight Run to Baltimore

When I grow rich, I shall take a train whenever I wish, no matter where it's going. The very rich travel in drawing rooms, the very very rich in private cars attached to the rest of the train. I do not plan, do not even wish, to be very (or very very) rich. I hope to make enough money so that when the longing seizes me, I can go to South Station and buy a round-trip ticket to anywhere, go there for the ride, and then ride back again.

I want always to travel by night, sleeping in a berth in the Pullman car, with the aisle curtain drawn and my clothes disposed on the little hammock and the window shade up so that I can see, as we speed through the dark, villages with lamp-lit houses and church spires, and towns with factories alight where work goes on around the clock, and long stretches of woodland alternating with lakes, with moonlight touching trees and water. There will always be a full moon when I am riding my train by night.

I want to feel the *click-clack-click* of the wheels, the hiss of pistons, as if they were part of my being. I want to hear, at crossings, the train's long drawn-out whistle, like the voice of an iron hound belling in the night.

I want to lie all night unsleeping, so as to miss no part of my journey, and think how there must be sleepless people in villages we are speeding past, who hear in their shadowed bedrooms the sound that I, in my berth, am thrilling to as the train leaves them behind and we go on and on, in the night, in the dark, in the moonlight.

To me, all that would be very heaven.

The day, or rather, the evening after my encounter with Mr. Groveland, I was on a train bound for Maryland and the hostelry run by Frederick Lindeman. Marcel and Shane Finley were traveling with me.

Miss Clara had decided not to accompany us. Mr. Lindeman knew her well, and our hope lay in surprise. More than that, I think she was so weary from grief, from rage, from months of waiting for the police or me to discover who had killed her dear Jewel, that to face each day at home was all she could manage.

She insisted upon my having a berth, as it was an overnight run to Baltimore.

"I should not dream of your sitting up, Miss O'Kelly," she said, in a tone more gracious than I'd heard from her before. She took one of my paws in both of hers, causing me to fear she might be feeling gratitude in advance of the outcome.

"What can I say?" she exclaimed. "That you should have solved the case so expertly, so ingeniously! Miss O'Kelly, I shall be indebted to you forever . . ."

"Please, Miss Clara," I protested, afraid she might come to regret all that graciousness and generosity, "I have tried to make clear that we are not altogether *sure*—"

"Oh, of *course* we are. Of *course* you are right. Why else would Mr. Lindeman have come here again and again, and once Jewel was . . . after Jewel was gone . . . why would he never come back, even once, to offer condolences? No, no, no. Rest assured, you have found my sister's killer and you and Marcel will go to Baltimore and . . ." She broke off, racked again by tears. "I know you will do what must be done."

Sobbing, she ran from the room.

For my part, I went immediately to police headquarters to explain the situation. There I found Shane Finley behind the desk, wearing sergeant's stripes!

His mouth fell open as he got to his feet.

"It is, it is! It is Eileen O'Kelly! Can I trust me eyes, at all, at all?" He thumped his chest. "You'll be observin' how I made sergeant, despite yer outspoken doubts, Eileen. So now, what do you say? Shall we resume walkin' out? I'll promise niver agin to use the hated phrase—" He winked. "You'll be knowin' the phrase that's in me mind."

"I'm glad for your promotion, Sergeant, and no, we shall not resume walking out. Put that from your mind. Now, you will please attend to what I have to say, or I'll find someone who will do so."

I'll give him this, finding me serious, he dropped the waggery. Sitting at his desk, he opened a notebook and gave me his attention. I explained about Mr. Frederick Lindeman and his hostelry in Baltimore, and how his visits to the Inn on Nashua Street had suddenly ceased.

"That followed immediately upon the murder of Madame Jewel. And the disappearance of her cookery book."

Sergeant Finley frowned.

"And yer sayin' that down there in Baltymore, this party is servin' up a dish he calls Oyster Bubble that Mr. Groveland declared was the precise duplicate of Madame Jewel's famous Oyster Puff? Well, well, well. I think we'd best pay a call on this boyo . . ."

The Boston police do *not* give up on murders.

That evening Sergeant Finley and Marcel and I were on the overnight train to Maryland. We had dinner in the dining car, a meal Marcel commented upon favorably, but which I scarcely touched, the thrill of the train being all the nourishment I needed.

Sergeant Finley was grumpy. Marcel was in excellent spirits, and there was something about him, now out of his enveloping chef's habit, that tugged at my memory in a pleasant way.

Something about him . . .

Dinner finished, Marcel courteously explained that he was *fatigué*. Shane was indulging in such huge, uncovered, jaw-cracking yawns that he couldn't explain anything. They would be sitting up all night, not having been treated to berths by Miss Clara.

I decided to visit the club car, so as not to miss any part of my first experience on a train. Mercy, how chic it was! Soft leather chairs, etched glass doors with brass handles, brass chandeliers all down the car, candles and fresh roses at each little table.

And such fashionably dressed folk! It was all so *haute monde*—so high class—that I felt shy, not a familiar sensation with me. Making my way to the nearest empty chair, I sat with head high and caught the eye of a Pullman car waiter.

"I believe I shall have a glass of sparkling milk," I said, my voice strained with the effort not to appear impressed.

Across the aisle sat a large Maltese cat, a gentleman with an air of lifelong command. He was smoking a fragrant cigar. Our eyes happened to meet, and as I sipped my sparkling milk, he smiled and raised his glass to me slightly. I smiled back and presently left the club car feeling just fine.

Later I lay, as I hope to do many times in future, in a cozy berth that had been mysteriously turned down in my absence. I gazed through the window, feeling the *click-clack-click* of turning wheels, the driving thrust of pistons, hearing with a shiver of melancholy pleasure the long wail of the whistle streaming backward in the night as we flung villages and towns and whole cities behind us.

I love trains!

In the morning, we went to the Baltimore police station, where Sergeant Finley explained the situation to a Captain Parsons. The problem was to prove that Lindeman had stolen the receipt book, and in the course of his theft had been surprised by Madame Jewel and murdered her.

To claim that his Oyster Bubble was Madame Jewel's Oyster Puff would be insufficient proof of guilt. Lindeman could simply say he had experimented until he found the right way to make the dish. Could we demonstrate otherwise?

No—we were obliged to find the book itself, and that might not be easy. If we did find it, of course it would be impossible for Lindeman to explain its being in his possession, and we would have him.

"Per'aps," Marcel had suggested, "'e has disposed of it. Would that not be *prudent?* I mean, very wise? After 'e copies down directions for *la Puffe,* then *poof*—away with it into the Bay of Chesapeake! Would not this book be *très difficile* to explain if found?" he demanded of Shane Finley.

"Why would he expect it to be found, then? Here he is in Baltymore, snug as a Kerry cow, thinkin' no doubt that the hunt fer Miss Jewel Ramsey's killer is over fer lack of hints and clues and suchlike, unaware that the Boston peelers—I mean police—don't give up on a manhunt when it's murder itself been done."

"But why did Monsieur Lindeman knock out the aggressible Conrad? *Pourquoi?* There was Madame Jewel, dead in the parlor, and there 'e was with the receipt book under 'is arm. *Le voilà!* Off 'e is free to go. Knowing 'e is the guest of the Inn, Conrad would not stop 'im. Why, then, render the *la pauvre oie* senseless?"

Shane looked at me. "And what the—heck—is a povwaw when it's in Boston?"

"A poor goose," I explained.

"Why don't he say so?"

"He thought he had," I said, adding quickly, "I can explain about Conrad, I think. Mr. Lindeman knew that a stranger going in or out of the Inn could not escape the guard goose. Only a guest could pass that creature unmolested, and since it had to look like an outside job, it was necessary to—to render the povwaw senseless."

"Eh, *voilà,*" Marcel burst out. "Monsieur Lindeman, 'e stays the night, leaves very early the next day, per'aps at dawn, the purloined book safe in 'is valise, and no one the wiser!"

He gave the sergeant a triumphant smile, and me a warm and winning one.

So far as Marcel was concerned, the more I was in his company, the less justice I found in Miss Clara's estimate of him as lacking in serenity. He seemed to me admirably poised. And yes . . . most amiable.

Captain Parsons, of the Baltimore police, listened intently to our story and said the Baltimore police would gladly cooperate with us in so important a matter. It was settled that Sergeant Finley, Marcel, and I would stay at a nearby hotel and go to The Mariner and His Mate for dinner. Only Marcel would order the Oyster Bubble, as only he would know if it was the right receipt. (Or recipe. It had got so I didn't know what to call it.) Moreover, we did not wish to arouse suspicion by appearing unduly interested in a particular dish.

Captain Parsons and one of his men, Sergeant Burke, would dine at a different table, keeping close watch for any sign from us. They, like Shane Finley, would be in plain clothes. We wanted no uniforms to alarm Mr. Lindeman, if in truth he was the culprit and therefore alarmable.

Evening came, and Sergeant Finley, Marcel, and I arrived at the hostelry in a downpour. The establishment was a large, gray-shingled building right on the water. It was all alight, with the painted wooden sign that had impressed Mr. Groveland swinging and creaking over the door. It depicted a sailor peering through his spyglass, but no mate.

It was a handsome sign, but who knew what The Mariner had been up to before he opened his fine-looking restaurant? And was there really a Mate?

Well, we'd soon know. Or I hoped we would.

11

The Mariner
and His Mate

At the dining entrance to the hostelry, we stood a moment, looking around.

"Classy, b'gob," said Shane Finley.

Pretentious would have been my word. Overornate, compared to the simple perfection of the Inn on Nashua Street, as once it had been, and might, with good fortune, be again.

I noticed that Captain Parsons and Sergeant Burke of the Baltimore constabulary had already arrived. They were seated at a separate table nearby, ready to assist us if—when—the need arose.

A stunning Burmese with long black whiskers and turquoise eyes came forward. She wore one of those slim, side-slit gowns that only Oriental cats can—or anyway should—wear. Of turquoise silk, it matched her eyes. Marcel's eyes flew open, and I took an instant dislike to her.

She led us to a table by the window, from which we

could see, through rain rattling at the glass, many lanterns strung along the dock and fishing boats pitching at anchor on the cold tossing waves of the Chesapeake Bay.

"Voilà!" said our hostess, handing each of us a large, tasseled menu.

Marcel looked up alertly. *"Vous êtes Française, Madame?"*

"Parisienne. Venez-vous de Paris aussi?"

Marcel nodded.

"Ah, très bien." She gave him a caressing smile and floated back to the entrance to greet an incoming party.

Shane looked bewildered, as well he might, and I explained that Marcel had asked our hostess if she was French. She'd replied she was a Parisienne, and inquired whether Marcel, too, was from Paris. When he'd replied in the affirmative, she'd said, "Ah, that is good."

Now I leaned over to Marcel. "I thought you were from Quebec," I said in a tone that caused Shane to raise his eyebrow whiskers.

Marcel shrugged. "People from Paris do not consider

les Québecois aussi bons que les Français. Not the thing, as it were."

"That is just silly!"

"Ah, Mam'selle. More, I think, is silly in this world than is not silly. But—" He glanced at Shane. "I think I may per'aps persuade this lady from Paris to let me in the kitchen if she thinks I am Parisian. I shall go into raptures over the food, explain that in my 'umble way I am also a cook. I shall entreat to see the place where *la cuisine* so notable is prepared. Once there, per'aps I may 'appen upon the clue! Or even—*avec un peu de chance*—upon the receipt book itself!"

Sergeant Finley turned to me and said testily, "Ask him to talk so's I can understand. Will you do that little thing fer me?"

"That might prove difficult, but I'll suggest it," I said, proceeding to explain that Marcel was going to get into the kitchen where such remarkable dishes were prepared and, with a bit of luck, find a clue, or even the recipe book itself.

"Oh yeah?" said Shane. "I'd like to see him try."

Just then a young waiter in fancy dress arrived, pad in paw, to take our orders.

Shane asked for steak, of course. I requested the crab cakes. Marcel, with a show of deliberation, finally addressed the waiter. "It is said that your *maître de cuisine* prepares a fine oyster plate. Oyster Crumble, is it not?"

"Bubble," said the young man, with a small show of enthusiasm. "It's our—" He frowned, tongue at the corner of his mouth, then beamed and said, "It's our 'piece of resistance.' You won't go wrong with that."

"Ah, your *pièce de résistance,* your most special dish. For me, the Oyster Bubble it shall be!"

"Frenchy, are ya? Like—" He nodded toward the entrance where the beautiful Burmese was welcoming more wet guests. "Straight from Paree, she is," he said. "Married to Mr. Lindeman himself—he owns this place which is one day gonna have so much class they won't let a guy like me carry away the trash, much less get in here duked up like a honest-to-god butler but they're just gettin' started, doin' real good but can't pay so good yet but the tips are. Good, I mean. Days, I'm a fisherman, most likely I dredged up the oys—"

He broke off, bowed too low, and said loudly, "Thank you, I'll have your order expedited in no time." He scurried off as a huge Abyssinian cat swanned up to our table, rubbing his paws together.

"Madame, Messieurs," said possibly murderous Mr. Lindeman, "welcome to my establishment. I hope all will be to your supreme satisfaction."

I smiled up at him. "Oh, believe me, Monsieur, that is our hope also."

He smiled toothily and glided on to the next table.

When our dinners arrived, Marcel took a taste of the Oyster Bubble. He scowled, took another, and growled, "This is Madame Jewel's creation. *Sans doute*—no question. It is her very *Puffe.*"

With a glance at Madame Lindeman, our hostess, he smiled rapturously, lifting his hands and his eyes as if he could not believe what he was experiencing. He put his fingertips to his lips and blew a kiss into the air.

She came to our table like a trout to a fly.

"You find this dish to your taste, *non?*"

"Ah, Madame! It is *sans pareil.*" He glanced wickedly at Shane Finley. "*Jamais*—never 'ave I tasted a dish so—so *magnifique.* Truly, your *maître de cuisine* must be a genius of rare quality!"

"*C'est mon mari,*" she said proudly.

"Ah, 'e is your 'usband," exclaimed Marcel, and she nodded happily. At that moment I became certain that whatever Mr. Lindeman was up to, his wife was innocent of it, poor thing.

"My 'usband, 'e prepares *toutes les spécialités,*" she went on. "*Les sous-chefs* prepare most of our dishes, and are of the best, but for what we call the Oyster Bubble, and our famous gingerbread with *crème,* also the sticky buns with *abricot*—for those, the touch of Monsieur is of the essence!"

"Madame!" said Marcel, as winningly Gallic as a cat could be. "I am, myself, employed as a cook in a 'umble way, and I think that if I could just be, for a small moment, in *la cuisine* where such miracles are performed, per'aps the littlest touch of the magic will translate itself to me. Do you think *c'est possible?*"

Madame Lindeman regarded the poor humble cook with compassion. *Certainement,* he could see *la cuisine,* though she deplored to say that where magic was concerned, only *mon mari* . . . and so on.

I gazed around anxiously, hoping the great chef himself was elsewhere. All during dinner, he'd been appearing and disappearing at intervals, but was not now in view. I hoped he was not in the kitchen. I hoped the *maître de cuisine* had gone to his quarters for a brief lie-down after executing so many pirated miracles.

Well, in short, Marcel did gain entrance to the kitchen, and a tense while later was at the door, waving one arm, Madame Jewel's cookery book under the other, Madame tugging at it and at him, meowing so shrilly that diners started from their chairs, goblets

toppled over, waiters dropped trays, and Mr. Lindeman came bounding from somewhere straight into the arms of Captain Parsons, with Sergeant Finley racing across to get in on the capture.

At the police station, Marcel and I waited outside the interrogation room, while Sergeant Finley, as a constabulary courtesy, went within.

They were in there so long that I fell asleep, my head on Marcel's shoulder. I woke to find him gazing down at me. Our eyes met, held, and for a breath-taking instant I thought he was going to kiss me. I think he thought he was going to, too.

Then Mr. Lindeman was escorted out by the Baltimore sergeant, and a moment I shall remember always was past.

"Where are they taking him?" I asked Shane Finley, my voice shaking a little.

"They'll be keepin' him here till mornin', when a magistrate is due. Then to trial in Boston, or I and me captain will know the reason why. It's a Boston theft and a Boston murder he's guilty of, and it's in Boston he'll be tried."

"You mean he *confessed?*"

"Couldn't keep him from it. Kept sayin' as how he did it all fer her—the beauty from Burma. He's head over heels and thought he'd no chance without puttin' on a big show. He don't own that place at all, at all—just rents on a month-to-month deal—"

"I wonder if she knows that," I mused. "She seemed so proud of him. Maybe she'd have taken him on his merits."

"Merits!" Shane exploded. "That's as nasty a boyo as you could shake a shillelagh at, and she's well shed of him before he could do *her* in, too, sometime when she maybe annoyed him, handin' him the wrong spoon or somethin' . . ."

He paused, scratched his ear, and continued slowly, as if not believing his own words. "Do you know, now, what he was after sayin', over and over, sort of singsong like some drunk that's lost the use of words . . ."

Marcel and I looked at each other in surprise, not having heard Sergeant Finley speak thoughtfully before. I said, "No, Shane. We don't know what he said over and over."

"He said, 'How was I to know she'd actually *die?*'"

Marcel put his head in his paws.

So far as my part in the case goes, I don't have one anymore. With, I grant, considerable help from Shane Finley and Marcel, I had uncovered the felon. Now it is in the hands of the police and the lawyers.

I'd as soon forget about it. But I wonder . . . will I ever see Marcel again? Surely he can't forget that he almost kissed me?

Well . . .

Case concluded

12

Christmas

I expected to spend Christmas day alone, which would not have troubled me. Cats require lots of alone time.

However, Mr. and Mrs. Groveland invited me to come round for midday dinner. That seemed pleasant enough, so I accepted.

Very early on Christmas morning, carrying my white skates, I walked to the frozen pond, across a field now muffled and silent in snow. A few flakes idled down, and from the look of the sky, we were in for a snowy Christmas indeed.

I was wearing an outfit I'd treated myself to with the fee from Miss Clara.

It's a soft lilac-colored cashmere, the skirts layered in tiers, the jacket tight-fitting, fastened with white silk frogs. It has a flouncy little peplum and is banded with white velvet at hem and wrists and neckline. With it I wore last year's Christmas present from Bertha, the floppy white velvet beret, and the big muff, to which I'd pinned a sprig of holly with berries.

I thought it a pity that there was no one to see me looking pretty in my Christmas elegance. But when I sailed out on the smooth expanse of ice, a whippy breeze at my back, I was content with the joy of flying through a winter morning faintly touched by the rising sun.

All at once, through a flurry of tossing flakes, I descried another skater swooping toward me. Bent at the waist, hands on his back, he advanced at alarming speed, then spun in a frisky curvet of ice shavings, stabbing his skates to a halt at my side.

"Mam'selle Eileen! 'Ow beautiful you are this morning!"

And suddenly I knew. I *knew* who Marcel had been reminding me of ever since my first glimpse of him in the kitchen of the Inn. It was he! Dressed in his checkered suit, his bowler hat, his scarlet scarf, Marcel was that magnificent skater who had sailed past, not seeing me, last winter on this very pond.

But oh, he was seeing me now, and the delight in his eyes as he gazed into mine filled me with such joy that I thought I might swoon of it.

I stared up at him, trying to calm my upstart heart.

"Eileen!" he said anxiously. "Something is wrong? I 'ave upset you?"

"Oh no, Marcel! You haven't upset me, at *all*. I am fine. I had a sudden—a sudden memory . . ."

"*Un bon souvenir?* A good memory, per'aps?"

"A lovely one. How good it is to see you. And how wonderfully you skate!"

"We *Québecois* are the famous skaters, *n'est-ce pas?*"

"Of course that would be so!"

"Vous permettez?" he said, holding out his paws.

"Oh, with pleasure," said I.

Paw in paw, we waltzed off together as if we'd been skating partners for years. As we soared across the pond, I felt my cheeks blush every time I glanced up at him, gliding so strong and sure beside me, his eyes when they met mine aglow with tenderness.

When, at length, I said I really must be getting back, Marcel allowed as he should also, this being Christmas day and a busy one at the Inn on Nashua Street.

"I'm surprised," I said, "that you can get away at all."

"One must 'ave moments of escape from the lady with the sting in 'er tail," he said solemnly. "I take mine early in the morning."

"Miss Clara's nature is unchanged?"

That Gallic shrug. "Does one's nature change because a great sorrow 'as touched one? Per'aps." He pondered a moment, then said, lifting his shoulders slightly, "You are right, Miss Clara does not change."

"I wonder that you're still there."

"Ah—that answers itself. Things have altered in the kitchen, and therefore in the Inn itself. I am now *maître,* with my own *sous-chefs,* my pot boys, and kitchenmaids. My *domaine,* in which I allow no interference. I can say that I am, at last, almost worthy of the shoes of Madame Jewel, rest 'er soul . . . 'ow two sisters who are twins can be so unlike! But let that go. Why 'ave you not come to sample my *cuisine?*"

"Because I haven't been asked," I said to myself, and then, aloud, "I hear the Oyster Puff is everything it used to be."

"*Vraiment.* In all modesty, I confess this is true. And I 'ave begun to experiment with dishes of my own. Not relying so much upon the cookery book of sad and violent memory."

For a while we skated in silence, and then I said, "Marcel?"

"Mam'selle?"

"A little while ago, you called me Eileen. I always call you by your name."

"Ah. May I, then, say *Eileen* at all times?"

"Yes, please. I should like that." A little silence, then, "Tell me, Marcel. Do you like opera?"

"Ah! *L'opéra!* I love the opera very very much!"

Hesitating still (was not the gentleman supposed to be first to ask the lady for—an encounter?), I said quickly, "I have two tickets to the—to a performance next Saturday. I wonder—I mean, I was wondering whether—"

His eyes sparkled. "Mam'selle! Eileen! You are inviting me to a rendezvous?"

"Well, anyway, to the opera," I murmured.

"I shall be *enchanté*. Which opera?"

"Tosca," I told him.

"My most favorite." He blew that finger-kiss of his aloft.

"Suppose it had been a different one?"

"In that case, a different opera would 'ave been my most favorite. The opera Mam'selle Eileen invites me to—that opera is my favorite!"

I was feeling so dizzy—so utterly intoxicated—with happiness that all at once I wanted to be alone. Joy takes me that way sometimes.

"I must," I said, sighing, "be getting home."

"And I must 'urry to my stove. Eileen," he burst out, "will you be my Christmas day guest at the Inn this evening?"

"Oh, fiddlesticks!" I said to myself and for a moment considered calling off my dinner date with the Groveland family. But no, that I could not. They were too generous, too kind to be treated discourteously.

"I should have loved it, Marcel. But I cannot. Mr. Groveland—you remember Mr. Groveland?"

"But of course! It was 'e who put us on the correct track to the—to the felon."

"He and his wife have invited me, in perfect truth, to spend Christmas day with their family."

Marcel looked faintly puzzled at how I'd put it, but shrugged, smiled, and said, "Then on Saturday, please? You will dine with me before *Tosca*?"

"Oh yes. Yes, Marcel. That would be wonderful."

More skaters were arriving as we walked across the field, now tracked with paw prints, I to my boarding-house, to rest before entering the Groveland festivities, and Marcel to take the two-mile hike back to his *domaine*.

Toward noon, wearing white boots, but still in my skating costume, I took a trolley that ran close to the Groveland house, which is directly behind their arboretum. I was, in perfect truth, on a cloud, in a haze of ecstasy, a dream of Marcel, and was at their door too soon.

A huge wreath of laurel leaves adorned with bayberries, bittersweet, lady apples, and gilded nuts decorated the door, and the sound of caroling rang out as Mrs. Groveland opened to me.

Well!

I could scarcely recognize in this plump beaming matron the frightened skinny thief of last summer. Like me, she was arrayed for the season, in a flame silk gown, a fringed green shawl. Still, it was not her clothes, but her smile, that made her greeting so festive. Such a smile in gray eyes that last summer had been tear-filled with terror was a lovely sight.

Good things happen, too, in a world where there is too much pain and affliction.

In the parlor stood a fragrant spruce tree, infinitely bedecked . . . popcorn necklaces, paper garlands, many charmingly painted wooden ornaments, striped candy canes, but no candles or brittle, beautiful German ornaments on a tree in a house where kittens came first.

A scramble of torn-open presents littered the room, and I gave Mrs. Groveland those I had brought for the children. Celluloid dollies for girls, tin soldiers for boys. I had thought briefly of reversing the order to see what would happen. But it would have been poor return for their happy hospitality to so infuriate their sons. The girls, I think, might've been pleased.

Mrs. Groveland presented me with a small, prettily wrapped parcel, and I was not surprised to find within yet another flacon of *Forget the Past.*

The six kittens that Mrs. Groveland had stolen to provide for were growing, but a kendle of four or five—more?—Groveland kittens was in evidence, at that stage when kittens are most appealing. Lurching about on legs still unsteady, tiny triangular tails held straight up, they leaped over one another, tumbled, sprawled, scrambled in furry confusion.

At the piano, Mr. Groveland was playing music of the season, while the older kittens stood by, yowling accompaniment. A fire fiddled in the hearth, and the odor of Christmas dinner, mingled with that of the spruce tree, was in itself a kind of music to the senses.

They were a family brimming with cordiality and affection.

But I have a low tolerance for merriment in a crowd.

Besides, I needed to be by myself to think about Marcel, to recall the intonations of his voice, to see again the vivid figure he had been, racing toward me across the pond.

I wanted to bask again in the recollection of his glance, to be alone in the warmth of remembrance, the promise of—what? I did not know yet, but something was ahead for him and me. Of that, I was dizzily, fizzily confident.

By dinner's end—a good old-fashioned holiday meal it was, with all the familiar dishes that are always relished—my head was spinning. All at once I had a sense of being suffocated by scents, sounds, squeals, meows, music, shouts of approval, gentle chidings for minor misbehaviors, and repeated assurances from Mr. Groveland that everything he said was no less than the perfect truth. He was, in perfect truth, an exceedingly talkative cat. Mrs. Groveland appeared to find it engaging.

"Well," I said brightly when at last we'd risen from the table, "what I think is that after such a sumptuous, scrumptious meal, and the music and the fire and the *conversation* and all of it—a brisk walk would be the very thing! What says everybody?"

My host and hostess exchanged hopeful glances, and I was immediately aware that the brisk walk was about to be undertaken by me, accompanied by the little kittens.

It seemed a fair bargain to take the bouncy brood off their hands for an hour or so, leaving them and the older children replete, relieved, and alone for as long as I'd accommodate them.

When the kitties were infinitely bundled and muffled in hooded snowsuits and scarfs and mittens and boots, we took off, I pulling them on their sled. They were so small, and the snow so nicely packed, that the trip to the field behind my office was a pleasure.

Once there, they tumbled off the sled, raced about making snowballs, and in no time were building a fortress from which to oppose another group of kittens that had been readying their own fortifications. This gang of kittens was too young yet to see a need to separate boys from girls. All together, they plunged into a boisterous, kittenlike snow battle.

In another part of the big field, a group of teenage toms was having a mock but all-too-real snow war. They were using, I knew from long ago, snowballs packed with ice, and they went at one another like gladiators. I looked away from them, wondering why fighting is so natural to the male animal.

I considered retiring to my office, to watch the activity from my window, but of course that would not do. I had taken responsibility for these kittens, and on the scene I was obliged to remain.

I did not feel obliged to remain in the line of fire, so to speak. Snow fire. A fallback was indicated. A retreat to the farther end of the field. Instructing my group— I was pretty sure it was my group—to refrain from maiming one another, I said I would take a stroll, but would have my eye constantly upon them.

Idly swinging my muff, I crossed the field where I had walked that morning with Marcel. I enjoyed the sound of snow squeaking beneath my boots, the sight of a black crow perched on a whitened fence post, the touch of occasionally falling flakes on my face.

"Marcel," I whispered. "Oh, Marcel . . ."

13

An Unexpected Discovery

At the far end of the field, I found another architect of snow. A lone female kitten, older than my brood, but oh, so young yet. She was working silently on a tower that was already quite high. It was pyramidal in shape and looked at once fragile and sturdy, like the builder herself. She was black, like me, with a streak of white down her nose. A face like a black-and-white pansy.

"That's a handsome structure," I said.

She turned, smiled. "So do I think so, too." With an air of triumph, she took an object from her capacious, not-very-clean coat pocket. Carefully, little pink tongue-tip protruding slightly, she placed this object precisely at the apex of her snow pyramid.

She stood back, eyed it for a long moment, then burst into laughter.

Well! I was laughing pretty hard myself. The sphere

atop her white structure was a dirty, cream-colored, infinitely scuffed, red-stitched leather baseball!

On a deep-drawn breath, I said, "*Where* did that come from?"

She gave me a sidelong, very nearly wicked glance, then looked across the field to where the tomcats were having their ferocious encounter.

"B'longs t' them. Some a' them as is fightin' over there."

"They gave it to you?"

She snorted. "*Gave* it to me! All they ever give me is a kick in the—" She studied my face, concluded, "—in the behind."

"You—ah, *took* the baseball?"

"Yerse. Those're me brothers." She pronounced it

brudders. "They found it outsida Furway, where the guy hit the home run everybody was talkin' about, last summer. You hear about that?"

"Oh yes," I said. "I heard plenty about it. How do your brothers come to have it?"

"Din't I just say? They found it. It landed on the street outside the park, an' they fought off everybody else tryin' to get it—they are *fierce,* they are. They took the stoopid thing home an' put it in their secret place. Under the floorboards in their grubby closet."

"I gather it's no secret to you."

"Not half, it ain't."

"And so you—"

"Took it outta there this ayem, fer me castle. This here's a castle."

"But Smokey Jack Slattery—he's the fellow hit the ball out of—"

"I know who he is," she said impatiently.

"Then you must know that he's been advertising and offering rewards for *months.*"

"Yerse. I know that."

"What's your name?"

"Floss. What's yours?"

"Eileen. Look, Floss—Smokey Jack really needs to have that ball back. He really truly does. It's his good-luck ball."

"Is it."

"Yes. It is. What good does it do you or your brothers to keep it under the floorboards? Or on top of a snow castle that'll melt, you know."

"Well, a' course I know that," she said scornfully.

"So what's to become of it?"

"They're holdin' it for ransom. They think. They knows all about how much he wants t' get it back, so

come Opening Day, they're gonna send him a note—
Pay Up or Else!"

"Or else what?"

She shrugged. "I heard them talkin', sayin' how they're gonna get home-game tickets an' balls an' bats an' anythin' else they want, when they get around to tellin' him they're the ones got his ball. They're makin' him wait. Suffer."

"Why?"

"Who knows. I jus' know that's what they say they're gonna do." She thought a moment. "It's how they are, me brothers."

"Why did you take it from their secret place?" I asked. "Are you going to—to hold up Smokey Jack, the way they planned to?"

"Nah."

"Then why take it at all?"

She studied me closely, then said, "I ast them. I ast an' ast could I play snowball fight wit' them. Oh no. There's six a' them, one a' me, an' they never let me do *nothin'*. So today when I said lemme play snow fight just once't an' I won't ask again, they tole me to go sew somethin'. That's when I decided."

"To get the ball from the secret hiding place that's no secret to you."

"Yerse. Here it is, right atop me castle, an' they'll niver find it, on accounta bein' too high an' mighty even to *look* at somethin' I'd build . . ."

She stopped for breath.

"My brothers were like that, too," I said. "Never let me get in on anything, no matter how I asked. I even begged, but they wouldn't let me."

"That right?" she said thoughtfully. "Maybe they're all like that."

"Some of them change, as they get older. Some of them," I said, unable to resist, "turn into Marcel."

"How's that?" she said incuriously, studying her snowball structure and its strange finial. She smiled again. "They'll go plain nuts when they can't find it. *Cuckoo,*" she said with relish. "An' then they'll start blamin' each other an' gettin' in fights. Not that they ever *ain't* fightin'. And I'll jus' watch them." She gave a sigh of pure pleasure.

"Maybe they'll blame you. Have you thought of that?"

"Me? What do I know about any old baseball? I'm jus' a girl, right?"

I got down to business. "See here, Floss, I'm a detective, and—"

"Fer real? A honest-t'-gawd lady gumshoe?"

Coming from her, I didn't mind the term at all. "That's exactly what I am. And one of my cases involves this baseball here. I can trust you to keep a secret?"

"Oh yerse. I can do that. A lady gumshoe. Don't that beat all. How come you to do that? I mean, be that. Can't be many."

"I'm not sure there are any. Except me. Maybe because my brothers never let me in on anything, either."

"So maybe you should thank them, right?"

Smart little thing, she was. But I shook my head. "I'm past thanking them. Look—let's make a bargain. I'll give you this—" I held my white velvet muff with the holly sprig on it toward her. "And you let me have the ball."

She looked at me suspiciously, seemed to decide I was not making fun of her, and reached out a tentative paw. "You mean—I give you their dirty old baseball, an' I get to have this here—this here—" Words deserted her.

I took her two grubby little paws and tucked them in the muff. "It's yours. Even if you think you'd better put the baseball back."

She continued to stare at me, wide-eyed. "Who cares about the baseball." She lifted the muff to her face, closed her eyes, and whispered, "I niver seen anythin' this pretty in me whole life. It is the mos' pretty thing in all the whole wide world. I'll share wid me mum, if that's all right."

"Of course it's all right." I was moved in a way unusual for me. "It's a lovely thought. And your brothers will get their tickets and balls and bats. Just to keep things honest."

"Who cares about honest?" Her little face was buried in velvet.

"I do. I'm a representative of the law. Sort of."

"Wonder what they'll think when tickets an' bats an' stuff starts turnin' up," she said, blissfully unconcerned.

"I'll have Smokey Jack announce that by a miracle he's found his lucky baseball, and to show his thanks he's going to give free tickets and balls and so on to boys who come to Furway Park on—oh, on such and such a day. Wouldn't your brothers show up for bait like that?"

"They'd show up fer a free peanut."

"Well, then. That's settled." I turned away, clutching the invaluable ball, then turned back. "My office is right over there, in that building, Floss. You could visit me, if you want."

"Yerse," she said, still holding the muff to her face. "Mebbe someday."

Recrossing the field, I prized my six kitties loose and took them back to their parents. I could scarcely be annoyed at having been saddled with them, since it had resulted in such an entirely unexpected—actually undeserved since I'd not done a thing to bring it about—solution to the baseball caper.

I sent a note to Smokey Jack Slattery, still in Cuba pitching winter ball, informing him that he could collect his good-luck baseball on certain easy conditions.

Case concluded

14

Springtime

Today is the first day of spring. In Boston, this means the sky is flat and gray as a sidewalk, an east wind shuffles across the Common, sneaks around alleys, roars down avenues with a knife in its teeth, and we look back with longing to the days of the January thaw.

But, for me, it is Springtime.

In a moment I shall explain why. But first to clear up a few leftover matters:

Frederick Lindeman is in prison. He testified, at his trial, that he was about to make off with the precious cookery book—so as to start a fine hostelry, thereby impressing the Burmese beauty he had fallen in love with—when Madame Jewel surprised him in the kitchen. She seized a carving knife and pursued him to the parlor, uttering threats. There he turned, grabbed the knife away, and drove it into her heart. He said it was self-defense.

The jury did not agree.

Floss comes by from time to time. She says her brothers are getting into fights, accusing one another of having made off with the baseball for purposes of private blackmail. She's getting no end of fun out of it. That'll sort itself out next month, on Opening Day at Furway Park. Floss and her mum wear the muff to church on Sundays—Floss going, Mum returning.

Smokey Jack Slattery wrote to me from Cuba, so

happy about the return of his baseball that he asked me to marry him. Ball players are certainly impulsive. I wrote back, thanking him for the honor, explaining that I was otherwise engaged. He won't mind. I do hope he gets his "stuff" back. He'd far rather have that than a wife.

One day last month, Bertha and I had lunch together. She wore a plain tan hat, no trimming. I guess she gets weary of her fancy creations and the women who come to order them. We had a good gossipy lunch, but I did not ask her to go with me to the opera. She will know why, when I ask her to be my bridesmaid.

I have not heard from the Vivaldis again, but hope that they and Tosca have found a place of understanding.

On the Saturday after Christmas, I was Marcel's dinner guest at the Inn on Nashua Street. Miss Clara stopped by our table, glanced from me to Marcel and back, seemed not to know what to say, settled for *bon appétit,* and walked away, her tail bushy with annoyance.

And then? Why then sweet Marcel reached across the table to take my paws in his and said, "Eileen O'Kelly, *je t'aime. Je t'aime beaucoup.*" No need to translate that for me.

"Oh, Marcel," I said, blinking back tears, "I love you, too. *Beaucoup* past measure."

He asked me to marry him, and I, in a mist of joy, said yes.

During the performance of *Tosca,* we held paws.

We were in thrall. To the music, to each other. Such beautiful music! Such tremulous emotion! On the stage, and in our hearts.

We have been to two operas since, but for me *Tosca* will always be the most glorious of all.

I have been in the office all day, arranging files of those cases I think, I hope, might make a book. Marcel is proud of me for attempting to become a writer, as well as for being what he calls the best investigator in Boston.

Looking these cases over, I recall how some were fascinating, some tedious, some even funny. I gaze out the window at the field beyond and think of poor Madame Jewel, the riddle of whose murder brought Marcel to me, and changed our lives.

We are getting married in June. Meanwhile, I try to put my records in order, in the manner of Dr. Watson. Will I one day be a published writer? Of that I cannot be at all sure.

Maybe Dr. Watson himself didn't know until he tried.

The End